The Rock Series: Book One

Kip and the Battle of the Rocks

J.J. Hansen

For Kip – my one true love – who knows the difference between right

and wrong and always chooses right.

Table of Contents

Chapter 1

I opened my eyes feeling rested, like the sleep after having had the stomach flu. You throw up and heave; your tummy keeps hurting; and you think it's going to last forever. Then, like magic out of a cloud, you feel better. Your mom makes you milk toast and fearfully, you close your eyes praying that the stomach ache does not return. It doesn't return, and the best darn sleep ever replaces the stomach ache. That's what it felt like as I opened my eyes that day in the middle of the pasture in the middle of the Orient Hills in the middle of Faulk county in the middle of the South Dakota prairie.

Quickly, something like fear crept into my moment of feeling refreshed. I was not petrified, scared stiff like petrified wood; and I did not panic. At that moment I was more alarmed like when the fire alarm rings in school. From atop the rock, I surveyed my surroundings. Nothing seemed to have changed. The pasture remained intact, its grasses swaying gently in the late spring wind. The prairie's hills still looked like waves, undulating one to another, like the tiny waves in the middle of a calm ocean. The word "calm" did not describe me though.

Prior to this, I never leapt from the rock. Usually this rock provided me with great fun. But, fear propelled me this time. I sprinted to the edge of the rock and leapt like a deer. Once off I stood staring at the rock, and I slowly backed away. I couldn't touch it, yet I was fascinated by it; so I approached it again. My brain told my hand to stay in my pocket; but my hand didn't listen, and I watched as my hand reached out toward the rock. I expected sparks, but instead warmth nuzzled my hand, like a puppy's furry nose.

That morning, I'd come to the rock as I always did, after checking on the bulls. As usual I'd climbed up, and I must have fallen asleep.

I spoke to the rock, "I must have fallen asleep."

For a moment, I relaxed and remembered how I had arrived at this place.

My assigned chore that morning had been checking the cattle. I loved this chore because my three-wheeler became a boat, and I rode the waves of the pasture. Pretending made my chore go so much faster because I had to count the cows, look them over for lameness, and make sure they had not wandered into Poindexter's pasture. After the chore, I'd find the rock; and the fun would begin.

Finding the rock challenged me, made me feel like Christopher Columbus or Lief Erickson. As usual, I felt lost on the prairie's endless waves, a ship lost at sea; but I knew that in the middle of this ocean of prairie, an enormous rock sat waiting for me. Really, major landmarks do not exist in the middle of the Orient Hills in the middle of South Dakota. But, I didn't fear, even though I felt discombobulated and couldn't quite place north and south. I knew that if I missed the rock, I'd find the fence-line, and then I could zig-zag back and forth until I'd find the stock-dam…or the rock.

Then, I found the hill. This hill descended into a bowl, and the bowl held the rock. The sight of the rock always stopped me in my tracks. I slowed the three-wheeler and gazed down at the rock. I grinned in awe that I'd found it, but, as I drove down into the bowl, the rock emanated an awesomeness normally associated with superheroes. The Incredible Hulk could hurl my rock with ease, for my rock weighed as much as my dad's Ford F-150 pickup.

Climbing challenged me too. I'd slip down the rock like a sailor on the slippery plank of a ship, but the rock's roughness had been known to skin my knee. No skinned knees this time, though. Once on the top, I laid back, arms wide open to the morning sky, and I smelled the history. The sun soothed me; the clouds mesmerized me; the prairie grass sang to me; and I fell into the rock and from within, the rock spoke!

A rock speaking, I thought, that...was one heck of a dream. My third grade teacher would love this, science and history all rolled into one. Great, I'd end up being the teacher's pet. No need to share this wacky dream. Keep this one to yourself, Kip.

I sat down in the grass and hit rewind. What had the rock said in my dream?

"To you, boy, I am a boulder, but to the enormous glacier that covered me and dropped me, I was but a stone. This great glacier carried me with care for over 100 miles. And slowly but surely, like a whittler of wood, she carved my bowl from this hill. As she moved away, she left me and the hills to ponder."

"Rock, what's 'ponder' mean?" I had asked the rock.

"'To ponder' means to think," replied the rock and then he continued his story.

"She was a good glacier. She carried me like a woman carries a baby in her arms. And when I fell from her, I fell lightly. But when a boulder falls lightly, it still leaves a mark. I fell into tall prairie grasses, and I dented the dirt here in Faulk county. At first, my resting place was a tight squeeze. On top, the grasses brushed against me like feathers, but in the dirt, I felt tight as a snake ready and willing to shed its skin."

"Rock, I've never shed my skin like a snake. I don't understand."

"To you, boy, it would feel like the tightness of a sore throat."

"Oh."

"For the first 1,000 years, tightness existed between the dirt and me. So in those years, I paid special attention to my surrounding, mostly to forget the tightness. The tall prairie grasses reached toward the sky, but I stuck out two feet above them. Looking across at me from the other side of my valley, I'll bet I looked like a bald-headed man. And, as I looked across my valley, I saw a sea of grass. When the wind blew, waves spread out like ripples in a pond. Above me, the sky lived. Most days, her happy shade of blue -- like the color of your Norwegian grandmother's eyes -- looked down upon me. But some days, her eyes turned gray, and she'd rain. Then the sky cried the loneliest cry, the cry of the sailor's wife awaiting her husband's return."

"Did it snow, Rock?"

"Oh yes it snowed. That first snow came at dusk, and I yelled to the sky with all my boulder might. 'Really? What is this? I am already tight, and now it is cold.'"

And the sky answered me, "Hush. Hush and watch it."

"So I focused on the snow coming down at me, and soon I was the warmest I'd ever been. At first I saw stars and snowflakes, but, without warning, the stars disappeared. The snow swirled steadily.

Sometimes, I focused on just one spot. For one second that one spot moved so fast with untold speed; the next second, it slowed and seemed sluggish but steady like a tug boat in slow motion. It swirled: slowly and then quickly…slowly and then quickly. Then it stacked itself like a deck of cards, and soon the grasses next to me bent as if bowing to royalty. As the grasses folded, the wind began to blow, and my valley became a blizzard…a blessed blizzard that mesmerized me to sleep, a sleep so deep that it seemed magical.

The wind woke me in the middle of night. Stars dotted the darkness, replacing the swirling snow. Now, coldness enfolded me, but I focused on the stars and the warmth returned, and I slept once again.

With the morning, came many surprises. First came a glorious light! Now, boy, this light was not the first light to hit the earth; I am old, but I am not that old. I know, though, that the first light might have felt like that morning's light. Though frigid, the morning light held the ambience of a cup of hot cocoa.

"Rock?"

"Yes, boy?"

"What does ambience mean?"

"It refers to the mood. It's how you feel when you've come in from the cold and your mom hands you a cup of hot cocoa?"

"I feel warm from the smell and then from the taste."

"That's how I felt when I was handed the morning light."

I had to pause in my memory of the dream. I looked up at the tiny clouds innocently pushing each other around.

Then, I couldn't control myself?

"What the heck! Who talks to rocks in a dream?" I hollered at the clouds. I felt my hands shaking; but I didn't believe the sensation, so I held my them out in front of me. I think, down deep, that I knew it was real. I think my body knew it was real, but my brain needed to catch up with my body.

To stop the shaking of my hands, I folded them in my lap. I stared at the rock. I suppose that I hoped it would speak. If it spoke out loud, then I'd know for sure. Then I wouldn't have to figure this out by myself. I waited. Nothing. Nothing but stillness, like an empty church on a Thursday afternoon.

Fine, I thought, Mr. Rock in the middle of a pasture, I will figure this out myself. I stood up and walked toward the rock. I stepped into the well-worn path around the rock. I recalled what the rock had said about the moat.

"My second surprise that morning felt wooly like a brand new Brilo pad. This mammoth rubbed up against me with a grunt and a thud. He rubbed with such force that I think he loosened me up just a bit, enough so that I felt a breath of relief before I fell back into my tight fit again. He rummaged around in the snow like a dog digging in the dirt. His trunk found the grass, and he shoved a trunk-full into his mouth. When he was full, off he wandered. At the top of my hill, he lifted his trunk and tooted goodbye. Then over the horizon, he went like a diver off of a cliff.

Once again I was alone. I learned what an eon was because I was alone for eons.

"Rock," I asked, "what is an eon?"

"Boy, an eon is a long period of time."

"Longer than a lifetime?"

"I guess an eon is probably two or three lifetimes."

"So, did you count the eons?"

"I tried. I counted the seasons. But sometimes, I just enjoyed the changing of the seasons. Once that snow melted, then that grass grew up around me again. Though humans equate it to watching paint dry, watching grass grow is an amazing miracle. First, the land is so tan, like unstained wood. Then the greenness peaks through. Its small amount causes your eye to think it is seeing things…little green spikes. Soon the green floods the brown. I watched the green fill my bowl and splash over the sides like too much milk in your cereal bowl. The green grass grew over the hill, and it grew up toward the sky again. Once again I was a bald head above the line of grass. Once again the grass blew in waves. Boy, it is no wonder that your Norwegian ancestors, lovers of the sea, landed here to homestead."

"The mammoth returned only once, but he brought friends. I tried to speak to him the way I speak to you, but I was still an infant speaking with an infant's tongue. Somehow, though, he understood that I needed him to rub up against me again, to loosen me up. Perhaps it wasn't my voice at all; perhaps the overwhelming weight of his wool had caused a horrendous itch."

"Rock, does horrendous mean horrible?"

"Indeed. He rubbed up against me again and once again I felt relief. The rock paused remembering and then said, "Delightful feeling! Both the mammoth and I felt relief!"

The mammoths didn't stay long before they headed west.

"Rock, when you were alone for eons, were you lonely?"

"No. Rocks don't get lonely. We sit on worlds, wonderful worlds. We have the privilege of watching both, but the voice of the prairie whispered to me constantly, keeping me company."

They both paused, both listening to the voice of the South Dakota wind.

The boy broke the silence. "Rock, so the seasons passed for eons. Then what happened?"

"My eons were interrupted by buffalo. The buffalo were smaller than the mammoths; they stayed longer and returned frequently. The mammoths and buffalo needed me for the same purposes, getting rid of itches. There were so many more buffalo than mammoths. The herd must have numbered in the hundreds, for within my bowl, there were usually 50 munching on grass; and they stayed until the grass was eaten."

"During their stay, the insects came out. Insects can't bug me, but they bothered the buffalo. Early on, one buffalo started stamping his hooves. I thought he was going to fight, but he kept stamping and stomping and before I knew it, he had broken through the grass to the brown ground below. It was the first time I'd seen the deep, dark, brown dirt; of course I'd felt it below me...for eons."

"For eons," said the boy at the same time as the rock. "Why did he dig?"

"He dug a wallow. He dug 15 feet around and two feet into the ground. Mud appeared. He stopped swatting bugs, let out a long moan, and then crashed into the hole. He rolled himself over and over in the mud like a baker rolling a cookie in sugar. Then he stopped and sat very still enjoying the mud bath, but more so enjoying the fact that the bugs weren't biting him. And then the other buffalo followed his lead. Soon they were all wallowing in the mud. When the mud dried, each buffalo had a mud coat of armor! For a while, they would escape the battle of the bugs. When you leave, walk west just a ways you'll find a brilliant patch of green; that is this buffalo's wallow."

"During the dry seasons, when water could not be found below the surface, the buffalo adapted and learned new tricks to ward off the insects. The mammoths would rub up against me to get rid of their itches. The buffalo walked around and around me...sometimes I felt like I was a merry-go-round, and they pushed me. They loosened me up quite nicely. For the first time, I started to feel comfortable against the dirt. The path became worn, so worn that they'd step down into it in order to circle."

I stepped out of the moat. I backed away from the rock and tripped over the front wheel of my three-wheeler. From behind the wheel, I observed the rock. Our cattle use this rock too. One time, while I was lying on the far side of the rock, a heifer came rubbing up against it. She was pretty quiet in her approach, but when she started trying to get rid of her itch, there was no denying her presence. I felt the rock shift, and I heard a low groan of a moo. She was satisfied, and she scared me right off the rock! So, Mr. Rock, the Hansen cattle explained the existence of the moat.

I spoke to the rock, "Obviously this moat was real, but the cattle explain its existence." The rock did not reply. I waited for a reply. I even snapped my fingers at the rock, but no sound came, only the slight wind across the pasture.

I needed to settle down in order to think. I turned from the rock and leaned my back against my three-wheeler's front tire. What had the rock said that would explain away this dream? I asked myself this question two times before my brain could focus. Then I remembered. The rock had said that there was a buffalo wallow to the west of the bowl. Earlier my brain had told my hand to stay in my pocket, but I had reached out to touch the rock. This time, my brain told my feet not to move; but my feet didn't listen either, and I walked up the west side of the bowl. I walked twenty feet. Those twenty feet were a numbed walk like the walk you take to the principal's office.

Bingo. Sure enough. The rock could not be wrong. A definite circle, about twenty feet in diameter, emerged; its football field greenness overpowered the normal pasture green that surrounded it. I found myself in the middle of the wallow. My open mouth matched the circle of the wallow, and I had to manually shut it. I couldn't help myself; I laid down in the wallow and continued remembering the dream.

"And then one morning, for what felt like no reason, the buffalo headed west up and out of my bowl. That night, it rained. The next day it rained. The next night it rained. The rain came for what felt like a week. Sometimes, a nice easy rain tickled my back, but sometimes it down-poured and smacked my back like a whip. When it stopped, rain water filled my buffalo path, and the dirt beneath me loosened up even more. It felt like clean bed sheets feel to you, Boy. Suddenly, a moat surrounded me; making me a castle in a bowl in the middle of the prairie.

"Soon teepees surrounded my moat. The Lakota had arrived in pursuit of the buffalo. When you wake, walk up the east bank of my bowl. At the top, you will find a chaotic ring of smaller rocks. This circle is a teepee ring. Carefully and with complete fascination, I watched the Lakota put up their teepees of 12 poles. The cover, made of buffalo hide, was then pulled around the pole framework. Excess cover was left around the bottom. Rocks were placed on the excess to hold down the edges. All the openings on the teepees faced east, and I wondered why."

The teepee rings! My brain hollered this at me mid-thought like a poor sport hollering at the referee. The rock said the teepee rings rested at the east end of the bowl. The numbness had left me, and a nervous run took me to the East. I arrived, breathless, and catching my breath seemed impossible. I scanned the eastern edge of the bowl like a sailor scanning the sea. I scanned three full times back and forth and disappointment set in like that sailor realizing that the island is a mirage. I sat, and the disappointment felt heavy like my suit coat, the one I have to wear for Easter and Christmas.

But from my cloud of disappointment, I remembered my Grandpa Jack telling me about teepee rings. When I'd asked him about the Indians, he'd said, "They were out there, out there in our pasture to be sure. Left teepee rings in three spots for sure. Probably more."

I wanted to believe that this rock really spoke, and for one tiny minute, fear left me. I looked for the rings again. You know those books filled with optical illusions. Sometimes you have to stare into them, into one spot, and then the picture jumps out at you. I did that to find the teepee rings.

I stood up. I scanned the side of the bowl again. Then I surveyed the plateau of the next hill; this plateau rested below the rock's bowl. I saw rocks. To see the rocks in a circle, I had to squint and then almost refocus my eyes. I centered my stare on the middle of the chaotic circle of rocks, and BANG, the ring appeared in its chaotic circular perfectness. I had expected a perfect circle. I suppose I thought the power of the rock, the magic of it would have those rocks lined up in a perfect circle. For a moment, I considered the nomadic tribe, the Lakota. Because they followed the buffalo, they would have to leave in a hurry. They wouldn't be concerned about where they put the rocks, so the left-over teepee rings probably never landed in a perfect circle. A messed-up circle made more sense.

The rock scores again! With the presence of the teepee ring in the location that he stated, I gave the rock more credit. A bit of faith for the rock took root in me. I returned to my memory.

"From the teepee closest to me, a young boy, about your age, stood at the top of my bowl. Instinctively, he scanned the horizon. After what felt like another eon, he found me with his eyes. His curiosity was evident in the skip/run/walk pattern that brought him to me. I thought that he would bound up with the same agility and speed that you possess, Boy, but instead he remained three feet away from me -- outside of the rain-filled moat -- and circled me like a predator. Several rounds into his circles, I realized he traced the patterns of the buffalo, that which was the life of his people, with his feet. Several more rounds and he reached out and touched me, running his hand softly around my mid-section."

"Eventually, he jumped upon me. His feather light weight reminded me of a deer. As he gazed across the bowl, he unplaited his hair which then found the wind and mingled with it. Soon he curled up in a ball; a dream sleep overcame him."

"Rock, this dream sleep, is it the same certain sleep that I feel right now?"

"Indeed, my Boy, the very same dream sleep."

"Will I wake?"

"When I command it, then you will wake."

"Was it the same for him? Did you command it?"

"His sleep lead him. In his sleep, he fell through me until he hit the vision world. There, he ran with the buffalo. He became one of the buffalo. He bumped up against them. Mostly, he thanked them for their service to his people. Just before waking and rising out of the vision, he saw the greatest vision of all. His tribe's buffalo kill would be sufficient to survive winter. From my mid-section, he reached out his hands in praise to Wakan Tanka. He touched my insides, but left his mark on my outside."

"When he fully woke, he sat up, scanned the bowl again, took a deep breath, and laid his cheek down against me. As he lay there, I asked him why the teepee doors all faced East. He whispered back, "The East is new life. The East brings each new day. We welcome morning. We welcome new life. Thank you, Rock." He raised his head and his body, leapt from me with deer-like agility, and he darted off toward the teepees. His vision quest did come true. The tribe left shortly in the direction that his dream foretold. When you wake, find the hand-prints that he left on my side."

Oh my gosh! My brain hollered! If I found the markings then the rock really spoke! I ran the run of a crazed and deranged man. I guess you could call it a stumble run. I suppose I looked like a puppy with my arms and legs getting tangled and my back-side trying to go faster than my front-side.

The rock had not told me which side. He had mentioned the mid-section, so I took that literally. I traced my hand around the outside middle looking for something. I searched for, what did the rock call it, eons. It felt like eons. I found nothing. I found nothing except the gravelly, granite skin of the rock. I sat down in defeat, hands drooped over my knees, head drooped over my chin. I looked up toward the top of the top of the rock. The wind rustled the grass and whispered, "Only ask," and so I asked. I asked it toward the sky, the blue sky filled with tiny clouds, puffs like the puffs from stacks of a tug boat. Slowly, I ran my eyes down the rock.

He said there were other worlds. If there were other worlds, then maybe his mid-section was lower. Before I could stop myself, I crawled in the moat and around that rock three times. On the fourth go, I found the spot, and no wonder it took me so long. The very faint marking, like a week-old kids' tattoo, came into view. I could make out the bottoms of the boys' palms pretty well. The thumbs were definite; the pointer fingers were fainter but still visible; and the pinkie fingers were an exclamation point; but the middle and ring fingers were barely visible. Maybe I could see those from the inside.

I caught myself saying that, and I realized that this morning's trip to the rock had brought me face to face with the supernatural.

Out loud, I stated, "This is outside of the natural order of things."

Then I paused, grabbed my head with both hands, shook my head between my hands and said, "Geez, I sound like a dictionary!"

I put my hand into the hand impressions left on the rock. I took my hand away and stared at it.

"Rock," I said, "It's me. The boy. Are you able to talk?"

I waited for his reply, but my ears filled with the sound of the swaying prairie grass. The gophers scampered around me, streaking from one hole to another. In the distance, the cattle mulled, and -- occasionally -- one bellered to another . Otherwise, silence. In that silence, fear overtook me again, and this time I could not move. I felt like my feet were super-glued to the prairie. I looked at my feet, but I couldn't move any part of my body. The screech of a black crow startled me, bringing me out of my paralysis. I ran the run of a crazed and deranged man. I stumble-ran to my ATV.

"Please start," I told it, "please start. Quit talking to inanimate objects!" I screamed as the engine roared.

I took off like a sailor and ship pursued by a water dragon. I roared on, until I remembered the teepee rings and the fact that rocks are everywhere in this pasture. I slowed down the ATV, but my mind raced on.

I told no one about the morning's happening.

Chapter 2

That night, I slept like a bike off its chain, waking up from the same sort of dream. I talked with the rock again.

"Rock?"

"Yes, Boy?"

"I know what, or should I say who, comes next in your story."

"Proceed."

"We come next. The homesteaders, my ancestors come next."

"Correct! And with the homesteaders, came the cattle. Never once was my ground broken for planting, too many rocks! But the cattle continued the routine of the buffalo, rubbing up against me, making me more comfortable, making the entrance to my worlds easier."

"I don't understand, Rock. Your worlds."

"Soon you will…understand. Peace be with you, boy. Until we meet again."

The dream calmed me until I woke up and realized that I, a human, did not normally talk to rocks! That's where the fitfulness occurred, not in my sleep but in my sleeplessness.

After the first dream, I walked out of my bedroom, down the short hall, and into the living room. Out the big picture window, the perfectly lined trees of our three-row shelter belt, planted by my grandfather and his brothers, blackened against the star-filled night sky. In the third week of May, 1979, the moon was full but beginning to wan. Once I adjusted to the light of moon, I could make out more clearly our large front yard and the tangled thicket mid-way between the house and the trees. Off to the left, across a pasture, were the distant lights of our neighbors. Off to the right was our machine shed, a big blue Morton building. In front of that was the birthing barn, where we'd been busy for the last two months calving out 350 head. Off-stage and on cue, a first-year heifer bellered to her newborn calf.

I sat down in the recliner, leaned back, and let my eyes wander from the lights of the Church's farm through the shelter belt to the machine shed and the barn. I felt relaxed. I closed my eyes...and then I dreamed again.

I slept on the rock, yet I watched my body from above; and I saw myself fall into the rock and disappear. Then the dream ended with the Rock's voice saying, "Soon you will...understand. Peace be with you, boy. Until we meet again."

Here's the craziest part of all: throughout the dreams I heard the Rock's voice the same as what I'd heard the morning before. The same. Dead-on. No mistaking that voice. The voice woke me. I sat straight up in the recliner. I walked back to my room. Climbing back into my sheets was nice, safe, and normal. My warm bed lulled me, and I kept repeating "Just a dream. Calm down. Just a dream. Just a dream."

Another dream started. I watched as an animal's claw drew a circle in the dirt. Even in the dream-like state, I knew it was the claw of a common pocket gopher -- that which I hunt and trap in our many fields and pastures. A voice -- not the rock's this time -- followed the circle.

"The circle represents Roxsthroe. Twelve other rings surround it. Laird rules Roxsthroe and beyond. Others, under Laird, rule the other kingdoms. Ringdom surrounds Roxsthroe, and Gerd surrounds Ringdom. Our enemy lives in Ringdom. He surrounds us and chokes us like an anaconda. Laird must get to Gerd and the other rings, but his secretive journeys have been intercepted. Roxsthroe finds itself in peril, battling against the menace, Geirrod."

As the gopher's claw drew the circles, I came to full understanding of what the voice said. Though dreamed, I felt as if I read a text knowing that a pop quiz would follow.

Then came the Rock's voice again. "Boy, you are a young one. From innocence comes uprightness. You walk upright, work righteously, speak truthfully. Tabernacled are you. Your trueness of heart will save both worlds."q

When the rock's voice woke me again, I shuffled into the bathroom and turned on the light. I turned on the faucet, let the cool water run over my hands, and looked into the mirror. My sandy blond hair was ruffled from sleep. Green irises stared back; green irises surrounded by a circle of yellow.

"What worlds? And, why would a rock talk? Why would a rock want to talk to you, farm kid?" I whispered to my image and then giggled quietly. "Enough," I said, "I will sleep."

But I didn't move away from my image. We stared at each other in a sleep-deprived state. I'd heard on this radio talk show – my dad loves talk radio – that a glass of warm milk helped people sleep. I left the bathroom and headed for the kitchen. The thought of warm milk without the chocolate sounded disgusting, so I drank it cold.

On my second trip out to the kitchen, my mom came out. Gently she put her arms around my neck and tossled my hair.

"What's wrong, buddy?"

"I had a bad dream."

"About what?"

"A rock."

"Oh. That's odd. Feel better now?"

"I think so. Milk, supposedly, makes you sleep better, and this glass is my second."

"That should do the trick. Let's tuck you in tight, so the bad dreams can't get into bed."

Finally, I fell into the deepest sleep. It must have been the milk and the hug of a mom. Morning woke me up with a start as the light lit the space between the curtain and the window sill. It slapped me awake, and then I detected the smell of my mom's homemade cinnamon rolls.

Chapter 3

You know how you hear that everything seems clearer in the morning light. As I munched on a homemade cinnamon roll, the plan hit me like a fast-pitch baseball to the ankle; only my plan didn't hurt as much. I would wait until mid-morning and then take off for the rock. I said to myself, face your fears. If it happened twice, then there was no denying. Denying what -- I asked myself -- that my pasture possessed a magical rock? Realistically, what good was a magical rock in the middle of the prairie?

I left the table a little disheartened, so I stopped thinking about the rock and focused on my chores. I finished and went to find my dad.

I found him in the shop under the swather. This swather dominated his time even more than the hay it cut. Haying season was nowhere near, and -- actually -- the cows and calves needed out to pasture.

"Done with chores, dad," I said and then quietly added, "Anything else?"

"Not this morning, Kip, but I'll need you this afternoon."

"Going over east to check the bulls."

"Didn't you check the bulls yesterday when you checked the cattle?" he asked popping his head out from beneath the swather.

"Yeah, but maybe I missed something."

"Better be checking thoroughly the first time," he said shaking his head.

"I'll be more careful."

As I took off on the three-wheeler, I wondered again, what good is a magical rock in the middle of the prairie? Having seen the movie *Jaws* and then the making of the movie *Jaws*, I felt I knew the difference between real and make believe. When I'd asked my mom about Santa Claus, she'd said simply and quietly, "You must believe to receive." That being said, I felt like the rock experience had been real, but -- once again -- what good was a magical rock in the middle of the prairie? The prairie -- like the middle of the ocean with no boats -- mostly consists of cattle, gophers, and prairie grass waves. Simply put, nothing exists there (part of the reason I love where I live), nothing that would require magic. I doubted myself again, but I had to try that rock one more time. I had to figure it out. I'd lain on top of the rock many times before, and I hadn't fallen into it. Who was to say that falling through it would ever happen again?

I reached the pasture and zig-zagged my three-wheeler. The rock sat in a bowl looking like a really large but normal rock. Like a forgotten baseball glove at the ball diamond, there sat the rock…right where I left it.

For the first time ever, it was eerie driving up to it, like driving up to a house that you'd been told was haunted. Ten feet away, I stopped and listened. Would I hear the rock speaking to me? The wind spoke through the grass. The clouds passed slowly above. The gophers wrestled, ran, and tagged each other before racing for their holes. Silence came from the rock.

Well, of course, I explained to myself, you won't hear it until you lie on top. You've got to climb onto it.

In the past, I ranked climbing on the rock first on my favorite activities' list; it ranked right up there with swimming in the dug-out, but today, it felt like the first day of kindergarten.

Stop thinking so much, I told myself. Up I climbed as usual. From my perch, I discovered the same view. I laid my head back and felt anxious but not fearful. What do I do now, I asked myself? Do what you normally do, I answered. I had to think about that. Normally, I'd play on the rock. I'd pretend to be a Jedi knight. Lots of times, I'd do my thinking on the rock. Sometimes, I'd watch the clouds. Playing on the rock did not feel comfortable, and thinking, well all the thinking that I'd done for the past twenty-four hours involved the rock, so thinking seemed out of the question. Focus on the clouds, I told myself. Lie on your back and watch the clouds. Quickly, I found images in the clouds. One looked like my dog Frazier. He'd been the best farm dog ever; he loved to chase gophers, cats, mice, bunnies. Once he scared up an injured pheasant and then hunted it down. He looked so proud when he emerged from the ditch weeds with the pheasant in his mouth and dropped it at my feet. On bad days, he snuggled away the "bads." If it had been a really bad day, then I'd wait for everyone to fall asleep and sneak out to the porch where I'd sleep with him. I watched his cloud wander slowly across the sky.

"Can't see the black spots on your tongue, Frazier," I spoke to the sky. Yep, he had black spots on his tongue. The vet said that black spots meant good breeding, and, in my mind, that vet was right. Frazier was not replaceable. His golden fur was soft like silk and his big brown eyes sparkled. He never barked, unless he dreamed; but he loved to retrieve.

We lost him last spring. Watching his cloud, I realized how much I really missed him. What I wouldn't give to have him lying on our rock together like we used to do. Lying there, I knew in my heart that he didn't die. He must have run off, but, if that was the case, then that made me even sadder. Why would he run away? Life couldn't get much better at the Hansen ranch, or so I thought. I remembered the weeks of looking and looking and looking. We hoped and waited and looked some more, but he never came home.

I focused again on another cloud, made of four clouds stacked on top of each other. They floated together and then seemed to separate and then floated together again. Slowly, I lost myself in the clouds and in the remembrance of Frazier's soft, golden fur. My sadness over Frazier, my troubles, and my worries seemed to float above the clouds and disappear. I could not hear nor feel the wind. The sounds of the wrestling gophers and the prairie's slight wind felt five miles away. Calmness came, and I knew what came next.

Falling into the rock felt like falling into the softest of beds, snuggling into the bed and the sheets and the covers, and then plunging backwards into the deepest of sleep. In this relaxed state, I realized I really wanted the rock to speak to me again. Really, I didn't want adventure. I wanted the rock to tell me more stories.

"Boy? Can you hear me yet?" he asked.

"I can, Rock," I replied with relief.

"Are you worried?"

"Nope. Just curious."

"I was hoping that you would return. I seek you. You are genetically predisposed..."

"Genetically what?"

"It means that you come from good ancestry," the Rock clarified, "and I can tell that your curiosity will make you a good adventurer."

"Good adventurer? Rock, where will I go?"

"I cannot tell you that, but others have visited this world," the Rock stated matter-of-factly.

"Oh my gosh! Rock, how will I get out of this world?" I asked because now I felt a petrified piece of wood.

"Do you know what a door knocker is?"

"Yes, Rock, we have one on our door at the ranch."

"Always look for the door with the hammer for a knocker. The door with the hammer for a knocker is an exit."

With that, I began to fall. Where? I screamed in my head, but silence surrounded me and left me breathless. I felt myself gasp, but I could hear no noises. I could not move. Though I fell, I felt at a standstill, as if up against a wall. I gasped again. This placid place where silence reigns and motion proves unnecessary captured my second gasp. My third gasp did not relax me, but it did not hurt my insides as much as the first two gasps. With the third gasp, I saw images: my family's ranch house, the rock, a door with a hammer for a knocker, my three-wheeler waiting for me.

Before I took my fourth gasp, I landed in the dark with a thud as my knees hit the floor. The ground felt like a weird cement, like cement with bigger stones mixed into it. I had to make myself breathe. I inhaled like a newborn baby, and when I exhaled I felt the pointed pain in my right knee. I dropped from the kneeling position to rolling in pain and clutching my right knee. I didn't cry out, but once again gasped in a breath from the pain.

From the darkness came a voice, "Is someone there?"

I said nothing...even in pain I became that petrified piece of wood.

"I thought I was alone, but, if there is someone here, then that would be fine."

I knew that at some point I would have to breathe again. This breath needed to be very quiet. This breath couldn't be a gasp.

Slowly, I exhaled, and slowly, the pain in my knee numbed. Perhaps the fear outweighed the pain.

In the silence, I surveyed my location. Darkness was everywhere. I couldn't make out shapes. But, faintly, maybe five feet from me, there was a small ivory, ghost-like creature. I could barely make out who'd spoken to me.

I could see him. Could he see me? What should I do? Speak? Silently and quickly, find the door with the hammer for the knocker and escape? Before I could make the decision, this tiny glowing creature moved toward me. His skin was a lamp. As he moved, I could make out the same strange cement walls. This room measured maybe eight feet wide and five feet deep. One wall held a door featuring no hammer knocker; instead a barred window let in no light. Great, I am in prison, I thought, where have you sent me, Rock? Just then, the small creature came clearly into focus. I, the greatest hunter of gophers in Faulk county, spied a glowing gopher several feet in front of me.

"Great! I've been dropped into a glorified gopher hole!" I spoke without thinking, but then I gasped.

Under my breath and mostly to myself, I said, "Rock, don't punish me for all of the gopher hunts. Rock, come on! In my world, gophers overpopulate!"

"Young One, you came from the Rock?

"Yes," I answered quietly.

"Then, do not be afraid. I may appear to be a gopher, but a gopher I am not."

"Could have fooled me."

"This is the Tower of Thorhal in the kingdom of Roxsthroe. I am your humble servant, Geirrolf the Giant."

"Whoa, whoa, whoa, wait a minute. First of all, gophers do not talk. I see a gopher. I hear the gopher. Great! Gophers talk. Second, a giant cannot fit in a cell this size."

"This," he said and motioned around me with his flicker tail, "is solitary confinement for a giant."

And with that, he crawled up the side of the wall. I had assumed that the wall ended above the barred door, but the wall did not end. Before I knew it, I could barely see the glowing gopher named Geirrolf. Then, before I could speak, Geirrolf bounded down the wall, stood right in front of me, and shook ever so slightly.

As he shook, I started to shake. As I shook, I realized that the floor shook too. I shut my eyes tightly; for the first time in my life, I did not sneak a peek. When the shaking stopped, I kept my eyes shut and my teeth clenched. Do not look, I told myself.

Then, faintly, and from the door, I heard a gruff voice, "Settle down, Geirrolf. You aren't getting out!"

I couldn't help myself; I opened my eyes. There, outlined by the bars, was a bearded guard holding a torch.

Geirrolf spoke, "Step back, good guard." This voice boomed and did not come from the glowing gopher. I realized that I peeked out at the guard from behind a gigantic pant leg. I had grabbed onto the knee during the shaking. I stepped back as if I'd touched an open flame. When I stepped back, I looked up…at all 24 ½ feet of Geirrolf. His head touched the ceiling.

In silence I screamed, Oh my gosh! This IS solitary confinement for giants!

And then I backed myself up against the wall, fearing the foot in front of me!

Geirrolf spoke again, "Are you aware, good guard, of what I'll do to you when I've escaped this tower? Good guard, I would give that some thought."

With that, the guard extinguished his torch. We heard his rapid footsteps as he descended, perhaps in fear.

I closed my eyes again, tightly, expecting to die when the giant shifted his weight.

The soft gopher voice spoke calmly to me, "Do not fear. I have shifted again."

My eyes felt infected with pink eye. Slowly, I peeled them open. First the right and then the left, and then I saw that Geirrolf was the gopher again.

"Never in all my life have I been so glad to see a gopher. Normally, I'd shoot you," I said without thinking, and then I started rambling, "But that's in my world where you've overpopulated our ranch, and we just can't get rid of you." I paused and then stated, "Never mind," hoping he hadn't been listening.

"I understand, Young One, but here in Roxsthroe we have few gophers, and most all gophers have specialties such as mine. I can shift-change into a giant when a need arises. This other world from which you have come, it is full of gophers?"

"Yes."

"Is it the land that we call Hansenville?"

"Maybe. My name is Kip Hansen."

"Kvist Hansen?"

"No, Kip Hansen. I know. I know. It is a weird name; my mom named me after a soap opera star."

For a few seconds, noiselessness spread like paint spilled from a can. I processed what had happened -- to me -- the bored farm boy. I found myself in solitary confinement with a glowing, talking gopher who changed shapes and became a giant. These three facts kept repeating in my brain: solitary confinement; glowing, talking gopher; giant named Geirrolf. Over and over these three facts repeated until I realized that I fixated on these two words: "solitary" and "confinement." I looked up and then down at the floor, and then reasoned that a bad giant probably got sentenced to solitary confinement.

"Your face looks muddled," stated Geirrolf.

"Excuse me?" My voice came out sounding like a squeaky toy.

"You fear my presence?"

"Just a little. After all, you talk, glow, and are a gopher who shifts into a giant named Geirrolf who," I paused, "has been sentenced to solitary confinement. Last time I checked, nice people, I mean nice giants, don't get solitary confinement." I tried to state this calmly, but my voice ended higher, like a choir boy's voice.

"Well, all I can do is tell you my story, and then you'll have to judge for yourself. Humans, giants, dwarfs, and elves as well as by creatures who have fallen through inhabit the kingdom of Roxsthroe. Chosen creatures can go between the kingdoms, creatures such as yourself as well as gophers and other small animals who have fallen. Our history swings like a pendulum in a grandfather's clock. It shifts like its mystical creatures: some generations have embraced the shift-changing and the chosen ones, and some generations have despised it and ignored it. Currently, the ruler of Roxsthroe is King Laird Thorstenson. He is a wise and kind ruler, and his people respect him. But, as with all good rulers, envious and greedy souls desire his throne. Laird's greatest threat, his most formidable enemy, is Geirrod the Giant. Geirrod is my TWIN brother."

"So, Laird captured you and put the brother of his greatest threat into solitary confinement?" I interrupted.

"No, not at all. Geirrod locked me in here."

"Huh?"

"My allegiance has always been to Laird. Once, as a young giant, Laird saved me. Therefore, I have used my ability to eavesdrop without being seen in order to aid Laird."

"Excuse me. What does eavesdrop mean?"

"It means that I can listen in on conversations without being noticed. Many a time, I have hidden underneath Geirrod's desk and listened to his plans. In gopher form, I can sneak into his castle and access his inner circle. I eavesdropped an important message exchanged between Geirrod and his Dorg."

"What's a Dorg?"

"A Dorg is a secret messenger. His messenger is a shape-shifter like me. The day that Laird and I discussed his secret journey into the third ring is the day that I knew for sure who and what Geirrod's Dorg was."

"Wait a minute. What is the third ring?"

Geirrod the gopher increased his glow just a bit. He used his paw to draw a picture in the dirt on the floor of the cell. He drew a small circle first.

"Deja vu," I whispered, "I know this story. I know about the twelve rings of Roxsthroe."

"How?"

"You," I said pointing at his claw," drew the kingdoms in the dirt during my dream last night."

Geirrolf crinkled his brow.

Twelve kingdoms surround Roxsthroe: Ringdom, ruled by Geirrod, and Gerd, ruled by you."

"Yes. Correct."

"You rule, yet you are brothers? Does your family own two kingdoms? In my land, we can own two farm sites, but we ranchers don't rule our land. Is it similar to owning two ranches?" I asked, almost talking myself into understanding.

"Quite similar, Young One. My mother, Grid, and her parents ruled the third kingdom, Gerd. She married my father, Gein, whose parents ruled Ringdom. Convenient, right? Together they ruled both kingdoms well, except for a short time when my brother put a spell on my father. That story will have to wait for another day," he stated, eyes rolling toward the ceiling.

Then he continued, "I love the part of my brother, Geirrod, that is good and kind. I love the brother of our early childhood, but something has possessed him and at certain times, greed and evil overtake his nature. I have spent half of my life correcting his evil ways," he finished and again he looked toward the ceiling.

"When my parents died, I inherited the outer ring, Gerd, and Geirrod inherited the inner ring, Ringdom, which puts him between Laird and me.

"So, Laird and Roxsthroe are surrounded by one enemy ring," I stated.

"It would seem," said Geirrolf quietly, "that what you say is true. In order to get to Gerd and Dadivland, the third and fourth kingdoms, as well as the other rings, Laird has to make secretive journeys through Ringdom. It has been these journeys that have kept him enthroned. Had the Dorg not discovered these routes, then I wouldn't be here."

"I still don't understand what a Dorg is."

"On the very edge of Roxsthroe, there is a substantial bit of land owned by a farmer named Frigmund. Fridmund's land extends through Ringdom and Gerd. Frigmund's dog is Geirrod's Dorg. He secretly belongs to Geirrod."

"Stupid dog!" I spoke loudly.

Geirrolf hushed me and said, "Do not blame the dog. The dog's allegiance to Geirrod is forced. Frigmund's land extends from Roxsthroe, through Ringdom, and into Gerd. Geirrod correctly presumed that Laird used Frigmund's land as safe passage; indeed, Frigmund possesses loyalty to the king, and Laird traveled via Frigmund's land. When Geirrod discovered that Frigmund's dog could shift into a mouse, he knew that the dog came from the Rock. So first, Geirrod promised him safe return to your world, to Hansenville. When the dog realized that Geirrod could not return him, he quit retrieving information from Laird's castle. Then, Geirrod threatened the dog; he swore that he'd kill Frigmund, and this dog has great love for Frigmund."

I scrunched up my nose and my forehead, shook my head, and asked, "The dog fell through the rock like I did?"

"Yes."

"So the Dorg shape-shifts like you?"

"Yes, but not into a giant like me. He shifts into a very unique mouse with gold fur."

I opened my mouth to ask another question, but Geirrolf interrupted me and said, "Before I answer any more questions, I need to examine your left foot."

"My foot?" I asked and then realizing that I'd asked another question, I stated, "Sorry. I didn't mean to ask another question"

I did as I was told not out of fear but out of curiosity.

Geirrod lifted my foot, examined the space between my toes like a gardener searching through his strawberry patch. Then he popped my foot up into the air with the speed of a football punter. He ran his hand along my heel searching.

I'd had enough, "What are you looking for?"

"A brown mark."

"Well," I said, "then you have the wrong foot." And with that I took off my right shoe. A brown birth mark can be found in the middle of my foot, evenly-spaced between my big toe and my heel. My mother had fussed about it. She'd even taken me in to see the doctor. Just a birthmark. Nothing to worry about...until now. Having ripped off my shoe and sock to show the birth mark to the giant, I realized what I may have set into motion.

I did not fear Geirrolf; in fact, I felt a kind of allegiance to him. I probably should have been scared, after all I had fallen through a rock, but I didn't feel fear. Curiosity had taken over, like a toddler with a huge, cardboard box. Therefore, I didn't think twice about disclosing the information about the door.

"I don't know if this information will help or not, but the rock said I could get back to my world through a door with a hammer for a knocker. Could you come through my door to escape this solitary confinement? Maybe, in my world, we could figure out a plan."

Geirrolf, through his teeth, and in a voice quieter than a whisper, said, "We must get you to your door now!"

"What?" I said back.

"We must act quickly. You must return to Hansenville and never come back."

"Ah...okay," I whispered, "What does the brown mark mean?"

"Kvist, no time to explain. The door is not far, but we must be swift. You must never return. We can handle Geirrod."

"Never return? Why?"

"You, like the dog, could fall into the wrong hands. The plan is this. I will shift back into giant form, and I will get the guards to open the door. Then I will shift again. They will open the door to find two of us. This should surprise them long enough for us to make our escape. If we fail to escape, then they will surely take you to the King's quarters. The door with a hammer for a knocker can be found in the king's closet. You have to escape, even if they shackle you, understand?"

I understood the plan, but I did not want to leave Geirrolf. I did not speak this for I knew that he wanted to rush me out of Roxsthroe, only for my safety. In that moment of silence, I knew I would return.

"I understand," I said, with clarity of purpose. My Grandpa Jack always uses "clarity of purpose" when he is positive as to what he needs to do, and I had decided, without a doubt, what I needed to do.

Chapter 4

Geirrolf continued, "Before you happened upon this solitary confinement cell, I had been formulating a plan of escape, but now I need to figure you into the equation. At this point, your escape outranks the importance of mine. My original plan involved making noise and then surprising the guards with my gopher secret. Only Laird; Laird's mother, Linn; and Laird's wife, Elva know that I shift into a gopher. The bafflement of these simpleton guards would have given me enough time to escape."

"Geirrolf," I stated, "I have an idea."

"I am all ears."

I paused trying to decide what to say. What does a guy say, to a giant, whose ears are as big as a human child's torso?

Geirrolf must have guessed because he laughed this stupendous laugh, like the sound of far-off thunder building as a storm approaches.

All I could say was "Yes, Geirrolf, all ears plus one gigantic body!"

In the middle of the solitary confinement cell, Geirrolf the gopher sat back on his haunches. He tossed back his head as if to swallow a really big pill, and then thunderous laughter rolled from his tiny body. At first, the noise shocked me -- such a big noise from such a small creature -- but then I, too, laughed, dropping to my knees with both hands on my gut as if they were holding my bellybutton onto my belly.

When we were composed, I shared my plan. To my delight, Geirrolf agreed.

"But what do we do once we've escaped into the hallway?"

"You leave that to me, young one. Just be ready to run!"

With that, Geirrolf stood up giving me enough berth to hide behind his right leg. Again, he shifted into a giant. Then he pounded on the walls, causing an earthquake effect all around us. My feet trembled, and it moved up my body until my teeth chattered and my eyes couldn't focus. It felt like the Tilt-a-Whirl at the South Dakota State Fair. Regardless of that carnival ride feeling, Geirrolf's earthquaking antics did the trick.

Five guards approached rapidly. The largest, the one who reached Geirrolf's thigh, hollered, "Enough, Geirrolf, enough. You will force our hand, and we will call in Geirrod as ordered!"

"Actually, guard, I need you to relay a hand-written message to Geirrod concerning a misunderstanding. I will not stop quaking until you do my bidding. If you do not, then Geirrold will be called anyway. Either way, I win. If you take my note, then you win as you will be the reason that we clear up this misunderstanding."

An excruciating pause followed as the guard pondered. As the pause grew, I realized that, in the world of castles and kings, guards probably weren't the brightest crayons in the crayon box. As that thought struck me, the large guard spoke.

"You win Geirrolf, but just this once."

With that, the largest guard opened the door and stepped in; and I stepped out from behind Geirrolf's right leg. The guard saw me instantly, and in shock, he did not move but grunted, "Why do you glow?" Quickly, Geirrolf used his right leg and pinned the large guard up against the wall behind the cell door before the large guard uttered "glow."

The cement of the wall muffled up the guard's scream. I grabbed his sword, so heavy that I almost dropped it; but adrenaline made me feel like Superman when I lifted it. I lunged for the keys hanging from his waist. Then I spoke loud enough for all the guards to hear me, "I am a chosen one from the over-world. I glow with power, power that will be unleashed if you do not obey me."

Hearing the scuffle, the other three guards entered the cell with their swords drawn. Their shock -- like a dimly-lit bulb, flickering and about ready to burn out -- and their feeble stare reflected their lack of brains. Yep, these guards were not too bright.

"Up against the wall next to the large guard!" I tried to maintain the adult voice that I'd used when I picked up the sword, but my voice chose this moment to squeak.

Geirrolf reinforced my command, "You heard the young one. Do as he commands or his powers will be unleashed upon you!"

That did it. Having never seen a chosen one from the over-world but having heard the mythology about a chosen one, they scrambled up against the wall like mice bolting when a flash light shined into the granary.

Without being seen by the guards, Geirrolf shifted into his gopher form and raced out the door. With a magical dexterity -- a strength I'd not known before -- I lowered my sword, exited the cell, slammed the door, and locked them in.

Down and down and down we ran like down the steps from our old church's steeple. With only the glow of Geirrolf in gopher-form, I ran as fast as I could. As I raced, I realized that another glow had appeared...upon my body. In shock, I stopped; confusion rattled my body like a chronic cough.

"What's wrong?" Geirrolf asked.

"I am glowing," I stated.

"Didn't I explain that well enough?"

"You told me to grab the sword and make the statement, but you never said that I would glow!"

He turned and scampered down the steps. Over his shoulder, he spoke, "I suppose I didn't explain it well enough. Certain chosen ones glow, and this glowing usually denotes shift-changers. As for the glow, as soon as you enter into the light, the glowing disappears. Now, you have to keep running. No telling how long we have until someone discovers our friends locked up in my cell."

"I'm right behind you," I said, "Where are we going?"

"No time for talk, young one."

As we ran, I held one arm out in front to examine the glow. Fascination quickly replaced anxiety, and, as I ran down the steps, I continued to examine my ability to glow. Then it struck me like a ball peen hammer. I'd glow in the dark. In darkness, I'd be discovered right away.

The stairs seemed to twist down, like an endless nautilus shell. At the bottom of the stairs, we circled around and underneath some stairs, where a storage area emerged. Our glow lit up this empty area. In the far corner, Geirrolf behaved more like a hunting dog than a gopher. He sniffed each brick searching for a scent. Without warning, he threw himself against the third brick near the corner. Dumbfounded, I could not speak. I'd seen gophers do tons of strange things, but nothing like this. Five times, he threw himself against the stone, and on the fifth throw, the stone moved inward just a bit. I should have known: castles with hidden passageways!

"Geirrolf, had I known, I could have saved you a sore shoulder," I said as I aided him in moving the stone.

"No worries. Once I shift, the pain is gone. Now follow quickly and quietly."

A hidden passage revealed itself, and once inside, he replaced the stone, "If those guards follow us, then that storage area will leave them sniffing and searching but not finding!"

"Years ago, when I was but a boy and Laird was a boy-king, and there were no threats, we set out to build a tunnel system. Only Laird and I worked in the tunnels. We worked at night and in secret, and only two years ago did we finish. As we dug through the final section, Laird sighed, 'Let us hope and pray that we never need to use these in times of trials and war.' Well, Laird," Geirrolf spoke toward the ceiling of the tunnel, "I'd say we are at war."

He paused as if in prayer.

"These tunnels take us under the courtyard and to the princess's quarters. You see, the shape of our castle is that of four towers with the courtyard in the middle. We've just come from the prison tower. The other three towers belong to Aesa, the princess; her parents; and her fathers' counsellors. Each tower is connected by a bridge and thus the overall scheme of the castle is that of a square with a tower at each of the four points. We get to Aesa's quarters; then we cross the bridge into the King's quarters; and then we get into his closet to the door."

"Does Geirrod know about the door in the closet?"

"No. Not yet."

"Once I am through the door, what happens?"

"Different process for all, but be assured that the Rock will talk you through it, especially this first time."

And with that, a small and feminine voice spoke up from a short distance in front of them, "What rock?"

Chapter 5

"Aesa?" Geirrolf asked.

"That's Princess Aesa to you, if you be my foe."

"Aesa, it is Geirrolf."

"You are not Geirrolf. Geirrolf is a giant. You are a gopher. I will deal you a mighty blow unless your friend can save you."

"I am Geirrolf. And how, young lady, did you know about these tunnels?"

Around the corner, a brown head peeked out like a child from behind its mother's leg. In my glow, her brown hair glistened red. Her green eyes shot toward us like a bullet, and her mouth set.

I could not control my heartrate or my mouth, "You...are beautiful."

"So, I've been told. You...are glowing?"

"I know. I can't control it."

"Explain yourselves or be skewered," and with that she pulled out a sword almost as big as mine.

In the words of a four-year-old, I cracked, "I have one too. Mine's bigger."

"Size does not matter. Can you fight?" she bellowed, as she flashed her sword with the skill and dexterity of a trained soldier.

"Aesa, stop! He glows! He is chosen!"

"If you are Geirrolf, then prove it?"

"I cannot, but he can. He has the marking on his foot...and...he glows like me in my gopher-form. We need to get him to the door, the door in your father's closet."

For the first time in this encounter, she seemed confused.

Feeling badly for her, I blurted out my whole story, "I fell through the Rock. I am just a farm kid, but I landed in solitary confinement with Geirrolf, a gopher. When I landed, I thought I'd shrunk and fallen down a gopher hole. I shoot gophers in my world, so I was a little bit freaked out; but then this gopher shifted and I was face-to-knee cap with a giant. We escaped, and now I glow, and the Rock said that I could get home through a door with a hammer for a knocker. Won't you help us please?"

Her confusion turned into a smile. She hugged me and gushed, "You have come to save my land. Grandma Linn said you would come. Bless you, chosen one."

The hug felt so nice that I almost didn't understand the words. Once again (she had this effect on me), I spoke without thinking, "I can't save your world. I am just a farm kid. And besides, Geirrolf said that I needed to go home and never return."

"But," she said in a confident whisper, "you will return. Let us have proper introductions. I am Aesa Linnley Cecille Thorstenson," she said this and curtsied.

"Kip John Hansen. Pleased to make your acquaintance," I said bowing and sounding like an adult.

"We sound silly," she said.

"Like our parents," I said.

"Oh no! We sound like adults," she said and we broke into this ridiculous fit of laughter.

Finally, I said, "I don't know why we're laughing so hard. Not that funny."

And she said, "I know what you mean. Not that funny at all, but it sure felt good to laugh like that. I've had such a time with my father in jail and my mother and grandmother exiled to the twelfth kingdom."

"Where do they keep your father?" I asked.

"I do not know. All I know is that I've been commanded by Geirrod to remain in my quarters or he'll kill my father."

"Then why are you in the tunnels?" I asked.

"I have to do something," she said and swung her sword around her feet, "and so I thought maybe I'd find an answer in the tunnels. Indeed, I did find the answer here...you."

She turned her attention from me toward Geirrolf, "And you? A gopher? Amazing. You hid it so well. Does anyone know?"

"Only your father, your mother, your grandmother, and you -- young lady."

"Well, there you have it," Aesa said, winking at the gopher. "Geirrolf, let's come up with a plan and then head to my quarters. Oh, and by the way, I've known about the tunnels since I watched you and father finish them two years ago."

"You, young lady, are sneakier than previously thought."

At the exit of the tunnels, she turned to speak to me. Her green apple eyes sparkled when she looked at me, and it felt like someone whipped two green apples right at my heart. I didn't really hear her say, "Come quickly and quietly."

Climbing stairs to a top landing, we paused as Aesa peeked around the corner and down the hall to her quarters.

"It's clear," she said, "follow me."

All three -- the torch; Geirrolf, the gopher; and I, the farm kid -- glowed all the way down the hallway.

"Geirrolf, I know how we can get him...his name again?"

"I am Kip Hansen."

"He is Kvist from Hansenville."

She continued unscathed by the confusion of our double-talk, "I know how to get Kvist across to father's quarters." Then she left the room. We followed her into what appeared to be the biggest toy room I had ever seen stuffed with dolls, doll clothes, dollhouses, vanities and sweet smelling girl things, until we entered another smaller room. This room looked more like a workshop with tools and mangled wood pieces. From a drawer beneath the work bench, she pulled a plank of wood with rope attached to both ends.

"This should do the trick," she said and snapped her fingers.

"Ahhh, Aesa, I remember this well. The swing set we built while your parents travelled to the twelfth kingdom. Your presence of mind astounds me."

"What? A swing set will get me across the bridge?" I asked in utter confusion.

"Kvist, this is not your ordinary swing set. This is much larger than the swing sets in Hansenville. It operates quite differently than the normal swing set," Geirrolf attempted to explain the situation, but Aesa interrupted him with a challenge.

"Afraid of heights?"

I could hear the challenge in her tone and so I replied quickly, "Never! I enjoy climbing trees, roofs, and windmills!"

"Good, then follow me. Geirrolf, I can get us across, but I can't outmaneuver Geirrod. You must help with that part of the plan."

"Let us think for a few minutes then." Geirrolf, still in gopher form, climbed on top of Aesa's desk. He put his head down and appeared to fall asleep.

"This is no time for sleep," I whispered to Aesa.

"He does not sleep. Gophers take this pose when they need to think and think deeply."

"Not on my ranch they don't," I said shaking my head in disbelief.

Eventually, Geirrolf lifted his head. He and Aesa set about to collecting the items we'd need. As they worked, I couldn't help but ask the recurring question in my brain.

"Geirrolf?"

"Yes?"

"Could I ask one more question?"

"Yes, you may."

"The Dorg, the dog: how did he cause the downfall of the kingdom?"

"On that particular day, Laird and I discussed his travel plans in what I thought to be a secure location, but after Laird informed me of his plan and his route to secretly travel through Frigmund's farm from Roxsthroe through Ringdom to Gerd, I heard a noise in the hallway. When I stepped out to investigate, I saw a mouse. I walked back into the room, then thought better of it. This mouse was golden in color, so I shifted into gopher form and quietly followed the mouse. He meandered around the castle for a bit and then exited the castle.

The mouse sneaked across the moat by scurrying close to the left side of the bridge and then sneaked into the coverage of the Forest of Folke just beyond the moat. I briefly lost him in the forest and actually emerged before him. Luckily he emerged near where I hid myself. He emerged as that golden mouse but quickly shifted into his dog form. I followed at a safe distance.

He stopped at Frigmund's farm only long enough to find Frigmund. It seemed that once he was sure of Frigmund's safety, he then proceeded across the border into Ringdom. He followed a little-used, little-known dirt path to a "secret" location, a hidden cottage that resembled a miniature castle. Instead of going across the bridge, he swam the moat. Clever, I thought to myself, he won't alert anyone. As a pocket gopher, I can swim, but I did not want to alert the dog, so I found my usual burrow and made my way into the courtyard just in time to see the dog disappear through the castle's closing door. I located my next burrow which took me into the front hall of the castle.

Once there I followed the gopher into Geirrod's personal chamber, and then I knew before he spoke that the dog was Geirrod's Dorg. From under Geirrod's desk, I heard the dog shift back into mouse form and speak. Geirrod's quiet malicious laugh whispered his corruptness. Geirrod spoke, 'Good information, Dorg. Your master, will live another day.'

Then he called his armed guard and his closest advisors into the room, and as they determined their plan of action, I could not control my anger. When I cannot control my anger, I cannot control my shifting. From beneath the desk, I shifted. When I shifted, my feet went through the flooring just like Rumpelstitzkin's when he heard the princess say his name. There I found myself stuck from my knees down, and I could not free myself. I flailed my arms in frustration. Geirrod, an astute and cunning man, quickly recovered his senses, and he had armed guards strap my hands behind my back. Then, all I remember is Geirrod coming at me."

"I assume that when Geirrod gained control of Laird's castle, he locked me up."

"So, Geirrod captured Laird?"

"It is true," said Aesa. "My father is held prisoner somewhere in the castle."

"Shoot! This is a predicament!" I exclaimed, pleased with myself for using a big vocabulary word.

"I cannot shoot, young one, I have no weapon to discharge," stated Geirrolf.

"I don't mean actually shoot me. It is an expression from my world. It means 'darn it.'"

The gopher tilted his head in confusion.

"Or like doggone...or dang...maybe drat?"

"Oh, drat I understand. Similar to confound it. When this is all over, we have so much to learn from one another," Geirrolf spoke with a smile.

I did not make reference to the fact that he had instructed me to never return. Perhaps, deep down, we both knew that I would.

Aesa spoke up, "This plan is a simple yet good one. I believe we are ready. We should be able to get you to the door quite easily."

The plan was simple, but the plan went a little wrong, starting with the fact that I had to dress up as a servant girl.

Before I could protest, Aesa had me dressed in the garb of a girl. My outfit included a large bonnet that covered my face. I would not glow in the light of the room; but during our travel there I would glow, and that could alert our foes, so the bonnet served as protection, a fabric shield to cover my glow. In addition, Aesa said the disguise served another purpose.

As I dressed in the closet, she spoke softly through the door, "This way Geirrod won't recognize you when you return, and I know that you will return! Also, if a servant girl vanishes in the closet during our brawl, she won't be missed."

While I finished dressing, Aesa and Geirrolf rigged the swing set, and I could hear them talking. As I watched them, I realized the first part of the plan. Outside Aesa's window was a zip line that stretched above and across the bridge between Aesa's tower and the king's quarters. Aesa and Geirrolf attached the swing to the zip line. As they completed their effort, Aesa said, "There!" with satisfaction.

"So," I said, "the plan begins with a ride across on the swing set. Then what?"

"Then we sneak to the door of my parents' quarters. This is where Geirrod stays since he imprisoned my father. Outside the door, Geirrolf shifts into his giant form," stated Aesa.

Geirrolf spoke next. "We hope that the guards have not escaped their cell. With the element of surprise, we can break through the door. We can hold off Geirrod and his counsellors long enough for you to sneak into the king and queen's closet."

Geirrolf continued, "Of course, you'll only have a few minutes to locate the door, but if I recall correctly the door with the hammer for a knocker hides behind a black chest. You should be able to move the chest and locate it."

"Well then," I said, "no time like the present!"

We loaded up on the swing. Aesa faced the tower occupied by Geirrod; Geirrolf climbed on my shoulder; and I faced Aesa's tower keeping us anchored to her window pane with my feet until it was time. Before Geirrolf gave the command to let go, Aesa, looking at me with those big green apple eyes, spoke, "Kvist, good luck. I know that you may not return, but do not forget us."

"Geirrolf, I know what you said that I shouldn't return for my own safety. But, I know that it is my decision to return or not to return. I have never met Laird, but after meeting his best friend and his daughter, I know...I...will...return."

Chapter 6

As I spoke "return," Geirrolf commanded, "Go!" I think that he meant to interrupt, so that Aesa would not hear me say that I would come back, but she leaned toward me and kissed my cheek as we raced down the zip line toward her father's quarters. The speed and the kiss gave me the most spectacular feeling like that feeling you get on the playground when you jump out of a normal swing at the very highest moment!

But the high lasted less than a minute, as we thumped up against and hit below the window to her father's quarters. She shimmied off the seat and climbed into the window. I followed with Geirrolf on my shoulder. Inside the window, Geirrolf shifted back to giant form, and we sneaked down a short hallway to the door in question.

"Now or never!" stated Geirrolf. Aesa turned the knob to the door, and Geirrolf kicked the door open and off its hinges. He stepped in, followed by Aesa and me.

Inside the room, I took my first look at Geirrod. Whereas Geirrolf dressed rustically and as a commoner, Geirrod sort of looked like a circus ringmaster; he even had the swirly mustache. He wore a red cape over his silken shirt, and his black pants were tucked into black boots. When surprise finally landed on his face, the swirl in his mustache lowered, and his mouth became a cheerio.

"How dare you!" he screamed at Geirrolf, but Geirrolf had the element of surprise. Geirrolf ran at Geirrod with the speed of a linebacker hitting a running back in the NFL. Geirrolf threw Geirrod across the room and against the wall. Geirrod was pinned, and he couldn't speak, for Geirrolf had his left forearm covering his mouth.

I scanned the room quickly and found two other giants. Aesa stood in front of those two giants like David before Goliath. She held her sword at them and said, "I have a small surprise for you. I have been a very good student."

Then she commanded me, "Servant girl, hold my sword!"

I did as I was told. Then, she held her hands apart like Merlin and raised them above her head. Between her hands, she formed a ball made of swirling fog. Using her eyes, she threw the ball against one of the giants and chained him against the wall.

"Cool!" I couldn't help myself.

She repeated the steps and chained the other giant before the other giant could shift his weight toward us.

"How'd you do that?" I asked.

"No time for explanations," she whispered. "Head for the closet."

She nodded toward Geirrolf who still had Geirrod pinned, "We haven't much time."

Geirrolf removed his arm from Geirrod's mouth, "Where do you hold Laird?"

"You shall never know, brother. You shall never know," stated Geirrod, and I heard his squeaky voice for the very first time.

Aesa stepped up next to the giant brothers, "Geirrod, you saw what I did. You know of my education in the Art of Mischief. I am not your match yet, but between Geirrolf and me, we can hold off your guards for quite some time. Again, where do you hold my father?"

"I thought that you said that you never wanted to see me again, Aesa. So glad that you changed your mind," stated Geirrod with a smirk.

Geirrolf slapped his cheek, turned toward me, and stated, "Get moving servant girl."

At this point, I started toward the closet door. As I walked, I noticed a mouse at the hemline of my skirt. For a moment, the mouse merely sniffed at my skirt. I tried to push it away with my slipper, but it persisted. Then, it begin to climb up the outside of my skirt. Now, I am not afraid of mice; I kill them all the time, but I did not want to bring attention to myself. I couldn't do anything until it reached the level of my hand, and then, I figured that I could swat it down. I did swat it down. It rolled down the skirt like when Jack fell down and broke his crown. When it righted itself on the floor, it began to climb up my skirt again. When the mouse was two inches up my skirt, I heard Aesa say, "Hurry, servant girl!"

Just then the mouse began to shake. Then, it shifted into a dog, my dog! Or at least he used to be my dog, Frazier, the golden retriever that my mom and I brought home from the pound. I couldn't stop myself, "Frazier?" I asked.

At that moment, the plan veered off course like an out-of-control freight train.

"What did you say?" asked Geirrod, but it came out as a command.

Aesa tried to cover, "My servant girl is a very simple girl. She speaks in odd voices and sometimes hears these odd voices too."

I recovered, almost sure that the dog, what must have been Geirrod's Dorg, was Frazier. The only way to know for sure was to see the dog's tongue because Frazier's tongue was covered with black spots. As I started to reach my hand out to scratch his ears, I heard, "Servant girl, enter the closet!"

I stood, frozen, with my hand half-way toward the dog. If this was Frazier, then I could not leave him here. I looked at Aesa; her green apple eyes propelled my hand back to my side. A sadness entered her eyes and made me want to cry. I knew that I couldn't be sure this was Frazier, but if it was Frazier, then this would be one more reason to return to Roxsthroe.

I turned toward the closet, leaving Frazier my farm dog behind; but, unbeknownst to me, the dog followed. Within the closet, I scanned quickly, but at the same time a ruckus began in the other room. I heard "Halt!" and "Unhand him at once!" I heard Aesa state, "Not so fast!" In that moment, I knew I had to make a decision. I found the large black chest on the left, but the bureau was on the right. The dog came in, moved slightly to the right, and turned to face me. As if on cue, he started to pant, and I saw the spots. I stepped into the closet and dropped to one knee. "Frazier," I whispered, and Frazier licked my face. But our play caused my bonnet to dislodge, and then I heard it, that stone-like voice.

"Halt! Dorg, retrieve!" At the door stood Geirrod. With a robotic reaction as if Geirrod possessed him, Frazier took my bonnet to the current ruler of Roxsthroe, "What is this? Step out servant girl. Step out immediately."

Before I could move, the door to the closet slammed shut. Before I could react, a man, who bore a striking resemblance to my own father, leaped forward and locked the door.

"No time to explain. You are obviously from the Rock. What door do you need?" stated the man.

"The one behind the black chest. The one with the hammer for a knocker."

As he began to shove the chest away from the wall, he spoke, "Then you have been chosen. Have you never returned through the rock?"

"No."

"Do not fear. The Rock's voice will find you."

The door was the color of cherries and the hammer was black like a night sky without a moon. The golden door knob stunned me for a moment, for I assumed it was pure gold. I felt out-of-sorts, a little numb, and frozen. For a moment, I looked at the man.

Then, I reached for the door knob and asked, "Laird?"

"Yes."

"Laird, I will go, but I will return to help. I don't know my purpose, but I must help you all."

"I know you will, young one. The knowledge of your purpose will come from the Rock and from your world. Though it appears abysmal, the situation is not yet dire. Rest assured and enjoy your trip back through the rock. It is the most calming of events."

And with that, I turned the knob and left Roxsthroe.

Chapter 7

I stepped through the door and off a ledge. I fell flat, a board falling parallel to the horizon. My fall gave me a certain strength, a hidden power, like Spiderman's ability to throw webs. It didn't feel like my muscles grew; I still felt like the same farm kid from Faulk county, but I felt empowered from within my body. I felt humble, like I'd been gifted this whole adventure.

Though I fell, I snuggled into the warmest of sleeping bags on the coldest of nights. It felt funny, like my mom was tickling my back, only she kept hitting my really tickly spot. I felt myself squirm, but that lasted just a couple seconds; then the snuggly warmth returned, and the feeling that my back was being tickled returned. It felt as though I drifted toward sleep but never quite reached it. It wasn't insomnia. I did not feel frustrated by the odd sleeplessness; I felt delighted; in fact, I snuggled in deeper and continued on toward sleep again.

As I snuggled in again, the questions formed like drops of water off of an icicle. Where would I land? What would happen when I landed? Could I tell anyone about this adventure? Would I tell anyone about this adventure? Would the rock let me go back to Roxsthroe? Did I really want to go back to Roxsthroe? Couldn't I just snuggle into this glorious feeling and sleep some more?

And then very quietly, the rock whispered as if he were across a room from me, "Young one, wake. Time to continue. Time to go home."

"Oh, Rock, I have missed you."

Very quietly the rock continued. "Young one, home needs you. You must return to discover your purpose."

"But Rock, how will I know?"

"You will know. You can do all things."

I spoke up one last time, "Then the first thing I want to do is get Frazier home. And I will pray for it every night. It is not fair that he fell through. He did not know what he was doing. He doesn't want to be a Dorg. He wants to be my dog, my farm dog again."

"How do you know this?" asked the rock.

"Well, it seems as though Geirrod has a strange spell on him that makes him robotic, dumb, and like a pawn in chess. When I spoke his name, it freed him for a moment, long enough for him to give me licks to my face. Rock, he can return, right?"

"Yes, he has a door, and he too can traverse the two worlds. But sometimes, things happen for a reason."

"What is that supposed to mean?" I asked the Rock with a rising voice, a voice that roused me from my restfulness within the Rock.

The Rock's quiet voice echoed, "Things happen for a reason...Things happen for a reason...Things happen for a reason..."

I felt myself drifting away from the Rock. I still felt snuggly warm, but coldness started to invade my sleeping bag of warmth.

And then, without warning, I dropped out. I closed my eyes and clung to whatever I landed upon. My hands and my legs, my feet and my toes, every appendage became a grip.

Aesa would laugh at this, I thought, and then I remembered those green apple eyes. With that thought, I pried open my own eyes and found leaves surrounding me and swaying slightly back and forth.

"Kip, what the heck are you doing up there?"

I looked down to find the laughing eyes of my Grandpa Jack. I looked over to discover the tree's branches swaying, and I realized that I had landed on the roof of my Grandpa Jack's house.

"Ummmmmm. Not sure what I'm doing up here."

"How'd you get up there then?" asked Grandpa Jack.

"Can't quite remember?" but the rise in my voice left a question hanging in the air next to me.

I turned my confused eyes down to my Grandpa Jack's eyes, and he said, "Well then, I see you've been to the Rock."

Chapter 8

I am old; I am not the oldest, but I am old enough to sense goodness and badness. As soon as the young one fell, I knew without a doubt that he would be what Roxthroe needed. Like his father, his goodness spreads from his littlest toe to his tallest hair. Cleverness and perseverance weave in with his goodness. These three strands are the braid that Laird needs to retake his throne, overthrow Geirrod, and overpower whatever other evil might be lying in wait.

The power in me was given to me as a gift, like life given to a human being. Long ago, the words started. Deep within me my voice began, and yet I know that my voice and my power were not from me alone. The power given to me is the same power that will lead Kip back to Roxsthroe and will lead Kip on his own land.

I am old; but I am sure, and I know goodness and strength. Though I am just an old rock, I am a faithful rock.

I am one of many stones on earth. Some use me to represent strength of character, and Kip will find that strength again and again in me and from me and through me.

Chapter 9

My Grandpa Jack went inside his house. I sat like a statue on his roof. I couldn't move; I knew that I should move, but I knew I couldn't. I suppose I looked like that famous statue of the Thinker, except I was perched on the top of my grandparents' roof. Truth be told, I suppose that I looked more like a boy perched on a roof than the thinker.

My statue state stopped when the screen door slammed and I heard Grandpa Jack say, "Don't you think you better get down from there before you roll down?" He stared at me for two minutes with his really serious stare; then he shrugged his shoulders, laughed, and went back inside. I followed him like an obedient pet.

I shimmied across the ridge of the roof, hugged the chimney, and shimmied around that. Carefully, I lowered myself onto the garage roof and crawled slowly like a reluctant combat soldier across that ridge, spotting my last maneuver, the trellis on the side of the garage. Halfway down the trellis, I realized that I used the utmost care. What's your problem? I asked myself this because I am a skilled climber, and, for the skilled climber, an A-frame house with an attached garage should be no big deal. I chuckled as I leaped from midway up the trellis. Safely on the ground, I looked back up the trellis and said, "Perhaps a magical trip through a rock would make the best of climbers a bit cautious."

At the screen door, I tried to gather my thoughts and my wits. I needed to know how Grandpa Jack knew I'd been to the rock. I could read his nonverbal language like a pitcher reads a catcher's signs behind the plate.

I walked into the kitchen. As usual he played solitaire at the table. I sat down in the chair next to him; but he didn't look at me, and he didn't speak. As usual the silence spread like softened butter over toast. That was one thing I could always count on; I always felt comfortable just sitting by him.

I looked down at my hands. Then I looked at him. His hair -- that same old buzz cut it had always been -- seemed grayer, or maybe I felt older.

"Buzzed because that's all you can do with that thick mat of hair," I'd heard my Grandmother Malinda explain my Grandpa Jack's choice of hair cut a million times before. His thick-rimmed glasses hadn't changed either. His lips -- thick and set together quite tightly -- brought forth the sound of his good-natured laughter, especially when he was winning at cards. I studied him like a football play because I knew I didn't want to make the wrong move. I waited for the perfect time to ask my question. I looked back down at my hands and waited for the right time. Quietly and without looking at him, I spoke, "Grandpa, how did you know I'd been to the rock?"

I asked the question, and then I listened to him slowly turn four cards over. It seemed like a week passed before the fourth card landed on the table. When he finally spoke, I think I jumped two inches off my chair.

"I'm looking for that darn ace of diamonds," he said in his loud voice, the voice he used only when working cattle and playing cards. Then, he continued playing as if he hadn't heard me.

A slight and uncomfortable silence stopped me from repeating the question. I looked up at him, and he gave me the serious stare again. Then he said, rather casually, "Just knew."

Knowing my grandpa well, I knew that I should let the silence spread again like softened butter on a bun, but I couldn't stand it. I blurted out, "That's it! You 'just knew?' But HOW did you know?"

He did what I should have done. He allowed the lull, and it lingered almost to the point of uncomfortableness; then he spoke.

"Your father used to land there now and again," Grandpa Jack spoke casually

"My dad?"

"Yep."

"He went to the Rock?"

"It was the summer of '38. Saved the farm."

Rarely did my grandpa string together two sentences. I knew I was pressing my luck, but I asked more.

"Did you see him fall through?"

"Nope, but Uncle Skinny did. Said it was like watching a puddle of rain water get soaked up after a storm, and, in '38, we hadn't seen much rain in a while."

I knew I shouldn't pause because I might lose him, but I had to gather my thoughts. I had to breathe.

"So how do you know it really happened?"

"I watched a giant named Geirrolf save your Grandma Malinda's life, and we kept the treasure that his queen provided."

And that cinched it up tight, like a saddle on a quarter horse. I let the silence soak over me. This silence felt really nice. It felt like the silence right before the final bell letting school out for the summer! I couldn't quite put my finger on why it felt so good. Was it the silence of Grandpa Jack's solitaire game or was it the fact that I now knew, beyond a doubt, that what had happened in the rock really had happened? And not only that, but it had happened to my dad too.

Without warning, Grandpa Jack lost at solitaire. He stared at the cards, but raised his head slightly, and then he snapped his fingers saying, "I'll get it next time." His fingers, the size of thick sausages and so similar to my father's hands, grabbed the cards and shuffled them neatly into a stack. He spoke softly, "Suppose we better head out to the pasture and get that three-wheeler home. There's a chance of rain, you know."

Chapter 10

I allowed the tranquil sensation of Grandpa's solitaire game to settle into my head as we drove toward the rock. It felt like the happiness that you get when you actually understand part of the sermon in church, and then you remember it for several more days.

I rolled down my window and allowed the cool breeze to soothe my face. Grandpa was right. It felt like rain. My thoughts scattered like seeds on the breeze. When the first drop of rain hit my forehead, and I wondered if it was raining in Roxsthroe; then, everything hit me like a full-fledged thunderstorm.

What was I going to do? I'd left them in a predicament, a tight spot. I'd left them, all three of them, in the sinister hold, of Geirrod. What could I do? The question swirled around in my brain like a tire caught in a tornado. This question caused agitation, and I withdrew my head from the window and reclined against the truck's seat. I tried to breathe calmly.

"It'll work out," my Grandpa Jack's voice spoke, but this time, for the first time in my life, his voice didn't calm me.

What could I do? What would Aesa do in my situation? What would Laird do in my situation? What would Geirrolf do in my situation? What could I do? The image of the smile in Aesa's green apple eyes while we formulated our plans caused the tornado of questions to continue rattling in my brain.

And then, it felt like like a soft and warm ray of sunshine entered my brain. The rock had said that I would find my purpose at home. I realized the question that I should have been asking all along. What would my dad do in my situation?

We arrived at the rock.

"Thanks, Grandpa, for the ride," I said.

"Be quick now, so the rain doesn't catch you," he said, and he snickered quietly. The snickering spread with Grandpa Jack's grin: so huge that it made his eyes crinkle; so tough that you'd better make sure you weren't on the verge of a swat to the butt; and so calm like waves of prairie grass.

"Yes, sir," I replied and smiled back.

He turned and drove out of the pasture toward his house. I paused by the rock and couldn't resist the urge. I reached out and touched it. Its warmth touched back, and without words I felt calmness. Perhaps this calmness came only from the rock, but I couldn't help but think of my Grandpa Jack's calm smile as he'd dropped me off.

The calmness settled in me; I suppose it landed in my heart, and I headed home. I didn't speed until I hit the gravel road, but even then I only increased my speed enough to create a small cloud of gravel dust. I needed to think about how I would ask my dad.

By the time I entered our driveway, I was ready to discuss this situation. I was determined to figure out my purpose.

I opened the door; I went through the house and then out the back door. I found my mom hastily grabbing freshly dried sheets from the clothesline. I tried to act normal, but my mom is very smart and could sense something was wrong. One look at me, and she said, "What's the matter?"

"Nothing," I replied, "I'm just done checking the bulls, and I need to know where dad is right now."

"Sure nothing's wrong?"

"Yep," and I purposefully nodded my head, moved it up and down really slowly, to make sure that she believed me, or at least she believed me for now.

"He is at the uncles' place. Tell him lunch will be ready when he needs it, and I can bring it over. He needs to let me know on the CB."

It took me thirty more minutes and another three-wheeler ride to find him fixing fence over at the uncles' place. That thirty minute ride gave me time to think about how I would ask him all of my questions. But instead of working on my strategy, I let my eyes wander over the land, the miles and miles of land. Flat, not like a pancake or a football field, because of the small hills, but flat enough that you needed landmarks to guide you because sometimes instincts failed. And soon I thought about my uncles and being raised where they were raised. We called it the uncles' place because Grandpa Jack had seven brothers. Grandpa, his two sisters, and his seven brothers grew up there, and they never really left. Technically, Grandpa Jack left, because he married Grandma Malinda, but he moved only five miles away from the homestead. The sisters married and moved as well, but the brothers lived in the house where they grew up, all seven of them. One time, I asked my dad what my great-uncles were like when they were younger, and he said, "They worked hard, and they played hard!" This was evident by the hill of empty liquor bottles that I found in one of their unused barns. When I asked my dad about that, he said, "Well, rumor had it that they were bootleggers."

"What are bootleggers?" I had asked, picturing pant legs tucked into boots.

"That means that they made and sold alcohol, which was illegal during the 1920s."

My dad was a man of few words and gestures, but when he spoke of his uncles' wild ways, I could tell that he was very proud because his shoulders lifted, his eyes widened, and sometimes he'd motion and make gestures with his over-sized hands.

I found my dad about half a mile down the fence line, which stretched out behind him like the number of questions rattling in my head. My dad did not scare me, though he intimidated many. He'd grown up pretty poor, but, as he always said, everybody was poor during the Dirty Thirties. But he grew up big enough and strong enough that many boys and men feared him! In his late teens, he was known as a fighter, but then he joined the army. After he served in the Korean War, he married my mom. Some said she softened him. Those who said that didn't watch him ranch every day, or they'd known that he hadn't softened. He'd taken that fighting energy and put it toward ranching. His hands intimidated me. He had huge pieces of meat for hands. I'd seen these hands yanking a calf from a heifer, shoveling food into his mouth when he was in a hurry to get back outside, pulling a tree trunk out of the ground, and grabbing the belt to discipline my older brothers. And I'd seen these hands hold my mom's hands making them look small as a child's hands.

Yeah, he intimidated most. Perhaps, he would have stayed intimidating to me, for I had seen him get angry quickly during cattle round-ups or when my older brothers didn't follow instructions or were goofing off. But, he didn't intimidate me because, with me, he was patient. Usually, I could ask him whatever I wanted, and lots of times that meant lots and lots of questions, and my dad would answer every single question even the tiniest, silliest ones. Granted, I had learned the right time to ask; one didn't ask in the middle of stacking silage or working cattle -- those were the wrong times. But when he was intent on a task -- like fixing fence -- then he allowed questions galore.

He followed the fence lines, looking for looseness. In the winter, snow packs into the fence tightly, like a well-wrapped Christmas gift. If the wire had gotten loose, then he'd get out the fence stretcher, attach it to the fence, and stretch the line back to its original tightness. Sometimes, the fence would get cut, usually by hunters out to kill deer. Cut wire was not so easy to fix. He'd have to stretch the two pieces and then attach another piece of wire in repair. Of all his necessary duties as a rancher, this one was probably the most important, for broken fences meant cattle on the loose, and cattle on the loose meant more time rounding them back up.

This fence line needed to be repaired today because we would be moving the cattle by the end of the week. Calving was over, and the cows and calves were being moved out to the green grass of the uncles' pasture.

As I approached him, I decided to ask my normal barrage of questions in my normal style: ask the question, give him time to think, listen to the answer, think about the answer for a time, and then ask another. But that isn't how this question/answer session went.

The nonchalant walk that I had planned to use turned into a run. I stopped just short of tackling him. He was on his knees facing the fence, and I heard him mutter, "Damn hunters." I stepped back, thinking twice about talking to him then. He heard me, and he looked up at me in a sudden sort of way. "Geez, you scared me," he said, "I was thinking about...."

"Sorry," I said, and then I stared at him for one full minute soaking in the fact that this man, my father, had been to Roxsthroe before me. Then, I hugged him, bear hug style.

And while his thick arms bear hugged me back, his gruff monotone voice asked, "What's this hug for?"

I pulled back, stared him straight in the eye, and said, "For saving Roxsthroe." And then I watched as his eyes went from hard as stone and intent on his work to soft like an over-easy egg.

"Oh," he replied, "you've been there?"

And he paused. At that moment, I knew this conversation could go either way: he could forbid me to ever go to the rock again, or he could allow me to proceed.

He looked across the field, paused as if staring at some far-off fence post, and then looked back at me, "Where'd you land?"

I sat down cross-legged beside him to tell him my whole story. He went back to his task muttering, "Idle hands are the devil's tools." He stretched wire while I stretched my tale. I know that I stopped several times to breathe, but it sure didn't feel like it. It felt like it spilled out of me like grain out of the combine and into the grain truck. When my story was finished, his story began.

Chapter 11

When my father finished telling his story, he went back to work on the fence. No applause, no showing off, only the usual air of quiet confidence about him. I nearly asked about the location of the gold -- the treasure provided by Queen Linn's tears, but I knew that would not be a good question to start off my barrage of questions. So instead, I reminded him, "I have seen Laird."

"I know," he said as his gloved hand twisted a connector wire. I didn't speak; I waited, for I knew his habits, and his habits were just like Grandpa Jack's: little talk but lots of action. He held the wire with his left hand and reached for the pliers attached to his belt with his right hand. As he wiggled the wire to cut it, he said, "Roxsthroe's in trouble, I guess. From what you say." Then he tucked his pliers back into his pouch and said, "Need you to stand back now." Knowing the routine, I stepped back. If the wires weren't secure, sometimes, they'd let loose like an out-of-control water hose. Slowly, he stood up, put his hands at the base of his back, and arched. Then he bent back down and stapled the repaired fence back to the fence post. Waiting for him to speak about Roxsthroe was agony, like waiting for your punishment -- your sentence -- after being grounded; but as he stretched, it occurred to me, for the first time ever, why he always took so long to talk, to spill out what it was that he needed to say. These long, drawn-out pauses gave him time to think. "What should we do?" he asked, and his question interrupted my epiphany. I cocked my head and looked at him dumbly until I realized the impact of that one question.

When he said the word *we*, I felt a wave of relief. I had faith in the rock, but now I had company.

I said, "I'm not sure, but I think I need to return there. Does mother know about your trips through the Rock?"

"Nope. Not yet," he said as he pulled off his work gloves. He walked over to the tailgate of his pickup. As he walked, the grass moved around his knees like a comb parting unruly hair. He laid his gloves on the endgate and said, "No need to tell. This all happened when I was your age." He opened his toolbox and put away the wire stretchers and the staples. Then he said, "I travelled back one more time to Roxsthroe. By that time, Laird's father, the king, was well again, and I could tell that Elva and Laird were in love. I left feeling proud of myself and what we'd accomplished. During that transport, the Rock said that soon I'd age and I would not be able to transport again. On my fifteenth birthday, I thought I'd try one last time, but nothing happened."

"So it all ends eventually?"

"I'm afraid so, Kip."

"Darn. I hoped you could come with me."

"Kip, I can take you to the rock and wait for you, but you won't need me. All you'll need from me might be the wheat," he paused and said, "Let's load up and head home for lunch. We have some explaining to do."

"But mom probably won't let me go back to Roxsthroe."

"She has to let you go."

"Why?" I asked shrugging my shoulders toward the sun.

"Because danger in Roxsthroe means danger heading our way as well."

With that, he reached toward his collar. He unbuttoned the top two buttons of his worn work shirt and pulled out a tiny pouch on a chain. He unfastened the chain and moved behind me. He refastened the chain around my neck. I looked down at it and back up at him. He grabbed my shoulder with his meaty hand.

"This pouch," he said, "contains the wheat."

Chapter 12

I didn't say anything to my mom; instead we proceeded through dinner as usual: "Please pass the potatoes. Please pass the butter. May I have more milk please?" I love pot roast, though food felt funny in my mouth, like I had a numb tongue and my taste buds had the stomach flu. After dinner, my dad didn't change his routine. He read the sports section of the newspaper as usual, and then he walked calmly into the kitchen, took my mom by the hand, and whispered something in her ear. He looked at me and said, "Your mom needs to drive me over to the uncles' place to get the tractor. We'll be back. Take salt out to the cattle and check those fences over east. Come Thursday, we move them out to pasture, so pay attention and look closely at each wire."

I nodded, but my brain moaned. He gives me a chore now? What difference did the current fence make if we were moving the cattle to pasture in two days?

My mom walked out the door. He followed but turned back to me and said, "It will give you something to do so that you can figure out a plan for Roxsthroe."

Then he smiled at me in a knowing way. He made me feel good like I had nothing to fear from my mom or from the danger ahead of us. He made me feel confident like when he'd quietly wish me luck before a wrestling match. This feeling of quiet confidence made me turn my head to the left and smile back at him.

I grabbed the block of salt and arranged it in the basket on the three-wheeler; I felt fine. I felt excited to return to Roxsthroe. I just knew that I could help them. I thought of Geirrolf; I thought of Frazier, my dog; and then I thought of those green apple eyes.

I checked the fence with care, looking at every strand of barbed wire, every staple, and every metal post. When I finished each side, I stopped and looked back, admiring the skinny posts set up in precision like soldiers. After I had finished all the sides and set the block of salt out by the hay feeder, I waited for the cattle to come. They rambled toward me gracelessly like I'd imagine Santa does when he runs along rooftops! As I waited and watched them, I evaluated the situation of Roxsthroe. I listed what I knew: Laird, Geirrolf, and Aesa were surely captured by Geirrod; Frazier, my dog but Geirrod's Dorg, was found out; and Geirrod was in control. I knew that when I fell, I would land in that same prison cell. I needed a plan. I really needed aid from the inside, but all my allies were caught, probably imprisoned in horrific ways. All I could really do was fall into the prison and hope that the guards were easily fooled once again. If only I could shift, I thought, and then I wondered a minute. Could that be a possibility? Frazier could shift. Maybe I could too. If I was stuck in a prison cell, then I might have time to figure that out; I had the wheat, after all.

I headed back to the house and waited. I knew that I would beat them home because bringing the tractor home was a slow process. Tractors can travel 20 miles per hour down a road, but that's paved. My dad would be traveling down gravel roads going 15 miles per hour with my mom following him in the truck.

Apparently, my mom did not follow my dad, because I looked up to find the truck barreling down the road.

My mom parked next to me. She jumped out of the pickup and was around the truck to me within seconds. My mom is the more affectionate parent, and so I knew a hug was imminent. Sure enough, she grabbed me around the neck because that's how tall I was. As I grabbed her around her tummy, she whispered, "So your dream was about this?"

"Yes."

"Why didn't you tell me?"

"I didn't know for sure. I thought it didn't happen. I hoped it didn't; but I couldn't explain it to myself, and if I couldn't explain it to myself, then I couldn't explain it to you," and then I paused and asked, "Would you have believed me?"

And she paused too. Finally, she used her index finger to maneuver my chin upward. She looked down, and her blue eyes stared hard at mine.

"I believe in a lot of circumstances. I believe in life after death."

"How can you be so sure?"

"I know. People die, but their soul lives on. Sometimes, I can feel my father, your grandfather, at my side. He doesn't talk to me, but I know that he is there. If I believe in life after death, then I can believe that there is a world beneath the rock in our pasture."

I smiled at her, and her eyes watered as she spoke, "It is a mother's job to question her child, and I question you quite often, don't I?'

I nodded yes, for I couldn't speak through the lump in my throat.

"It is a bigger part of a mother's job to believe in her child. I believe you, and I believe in you."

I don't cry much because I don't like how it makes me feel. I like being in control, and crying, with the chokes and the knots in your throat, makes you feel out of control.

I admit, though, that when we turned to walk into the house and wait for my dad, I had tears in my eyes, but these tears felt good, as if relief released itself into my body with each tear. She'd heard dad's and my story, and she'd believed!

Chapter 13

My dad and my mom drove me out to the rock. Though my mother worried (I knew because her eyebrows wrinkled, and she forced a smile), I had a united front standing behind me as I climbed up onto that rock.

My dad spoke, "Hurry home, son. We'll need you when we move the cattle," and then he looked from me toward the stock dam.

I listened to them as I watched the clouds. They discussed what possible calamity could be upon us. My eavesdropping did not make me nervous; instead it propelled me. I needed to save Roxsthroe so that Roxsthroe could save us.

Once again, the tingle took over, that tingle you feel as you snuggle in and start to fall asleep. I felt so snuggly. Once again, I welcomed the warmth of the rock like a cold nose welcomes the heat of a campfire. I reveled in it and waited patiently for the Rock to speak.

"Boy," the rock stated.

"Yes, Rock?"

"I am glad that you decided to return."

"I know."

"I like that you retain that quiet confidence."

"Rock?"

"Yes?"

"What does 'retain' mean?"

"It means that you possess it and have kept it."

"I see," I said and I paused. "Rock?"

"Yes, young one, chosen one."

"What will the seeds of wheat do for me?"

"What you will have them do," he stated so matter-of-factly that I felt like I could not ask a question even though I was confused. I squirmed just a little in my snuggly warmth, and again, I waited. Finally, I asked my question.

"What does that mean, Rock? What I will have them do is what they'll do?" I asked.

"The seeds will do what you will have them do," repeated the rock, and he paused for what felt like an eon. Then he stated simply, "You are not a rock."

"No," I said, "I am not a rock. Just a boy."

"You are not a rock," said the rock again. "Those seeds are yours, not mine. You are not a rock. You are not a well-worn path. What you are, young one, is good and deep soil. Those seeds of wheat, when placed in good and deep soil, will grow. Those seeds will do for you what you need them to do for you."

I worked chronologically through the rock's speech: "I am a boy. I am soil. I have wheat."

"How will I know when to use them?" I asked quietly.

"You are good and deep soil. You will know when and where to use them. You will have guardians to help you."

"Rock?"

"Yes, boy?"

"Thank you."

"For what, young one?"

"Without you, my father wouldn't have saved the farm during the depression."

"It was not I, young one. I am but a rock. I am an instrument. It was your father's faithfulness that propelled the salvation. I provide only opportunity. You, too, are good and deep soil, just like your father. Those seeds of wheat are your inheritance from your father."

"Thank you, then, for the opportunity, Rock."

"You are welcome, young one. Remember that you are good and deep soil...good and deep soil...good and deep soil..."

Chapter 14

I fell into the prison cell as expected. Quickly, I took my glowing body to the far corner, so I wouldn't alert the guards. I slumped down into my glow which extended two inches past my body. I didn't feel scared; I knew that I had to wait for something. While I waited, I pulled the pouch from my shirt. I emptied the wheat seeds into my hand and counted them.

"I have 60 seeds," I whispered to the darkness.

"Yes," the darkness answered me back, "You do."

I leap-frogged to my feet, nearly dropping the precious wheat. Carefully, I closed my hand around the seeds and looked into the darkness toward the voice.

"Who are you?" I asked.

"Who I am does not matter. Who you are seems to be the more important fact at this point. I see that you have some seeds. I see you carry those seeds in a particular pouch. Would you mind if I looked at the pouch?"

Using my other hand, I removed the pouch from my neck and held it out. While checking fence and depositing the salt block in the pasture, I had determined that whomever I met in the prison would probably be a good guy, so the voice did not scare me...only startled me. I dangled the pouch for what felt like an eon, a stout and very short creature approached. His cone-shaped cap looked like an old-fashioned dunce cap. He reminded me of the drawing of Rumpelstitkin in my fairy tale book.

"What are you? A gnome?" I asked, sort of out-of-the-blue, and as I asked it, I couldn't help but wonder if I'd landed at the North Pole. After falling through a rock, there was no doubt in my mind that my friends were wrong, and Santa Claus was real.

"Oh my, no! Gnomes grow to be only the size of a human's thumb. Wouldn't you say that I am much bigger? That's right. I am much bigger than a gnome. I am an elf, young one."

"What did you call me?"

"Why, I think I called you 'young one.' That term shouldn't offend, if you will, but does it?"

"No, not at all. I know someone else who calls me that. Please," I said, "take a look at my pouch."

His hands -- gnarled like the base of a big oak tree -- touched the pouch. For an elf, he seemed large but not overly-muscular. He turned the pouch over twice and stated, "You will need to remove your shoes." His tone turned serious, declarative, and monotone like a teacher about to scold a student.

"Ah Mr. Elf, I have been through this routine. The last time that I was here, I showed my markings to Geirrolf and Aesa. Please do not doubt, for I am a chosen one."

"I do not doubt that this is true, but I am a guardian elf; and, in order to assist you, I must see and touch the marking. As a guardian, we train to protect the chosen ones, but since Geirrod has locked all of us up, we have not been able to assist those in need," the elf paused but continued, "And no need to call me 'Mr. Elf;' I am called Egil."

"Pleased to meet you, Egil the Elf," I responded, "

"Prior to Geirrod's take-over, whose elf were you?"

"I belonged with King Laird," he said and suddenly his back straightened and his chin went up, "but I can serve two chosen ones during my lifetime: one from Roxsthroe and one from above. Now, if you could remove your shoes, then I could ascertain for myself, and we could get on with our plan."

As I took off my shoe, I asked, "What plan? How could you know?"

Placing a gnarled finger on my birthmark, he responded, "I did not foresee it, but the Queen mother knew it."

"Is she Queen Linn?" I asked recalling my father's tale to Roxsthroe.

"Why yes!" said the elf, "How do you know her name?"

"When my dad saved Roxsthroe, Linn and Lain reigned. King Lain, taken over by some sort of poison, had changed the rule of Roxsthroe, and he no longer allowed chosen ones to travel between the rocks: my rock and your Rock of Roxsthroe. Lain didn't know that his own son, Laird, a chosen one, had the ability to traverse the rocks; but Linn, seeing this odd change in Lain's behavior, kept Laird's chosen status a secret. Lain also changed the kingdom's economy.

Under the rule of Lain's father and grandfather, Roxsthroe was an agricultural state. They took from the land but always replenished what they took. Under the reign of Lain, Roxsthroe started mining for metals. This mining caused a flood. My father, King Laird, Elva, and Geirrolf saved the kingdom from the flood, but Queen Linn saved her husband from the poison," and provided my family with a golden treasure; but this I thought to myself.

"Indeed, you are well-informed. I never had the privilege of meeting your father. Lester, correct?"

"Yep. He gave me the pouch."

"I know. He has one and so does Laird. But the Queen-mother Linn and Queen Elva were in the twelfth kingdom when Roxsthroe was overthrown. They have been exiled there and have been commanded not to return to Roxsthroe under penalty of death. They hide in the twelfth kingdom in a religious castle, a sanctuary, if you will; but Geirrod is far from penetrating the twelfth kingdom..."

I couldn't help it. I interrupted, but, in my defense, my father's tale of Roxsthroe was still fresh in my mind, "Then, Laird did marry Elva? My father wondered that, but we assumed so because Asea's eyes are the same color as her mother's: green-apple."

I said this so fast -- fast-ball quick -- that I left the elf speechless. I felt the redness of embarrassment creeping up my neck and into my cheeks like a fever. I looked at my feet to gather my thoughts and then asked, "How far has Geirrod advanced?"

"OK, there you are, young one. My, my, my. We call that a tangent," said the elf in a persnickety teacher voice.

"A what?"

"A tangent, if you will. You've gone off on a tangent. You've veered away -- and quite a distance I might add -- from the topic at hand," said the elf. I lowered my cherry-red face and examined my dust-covered sneakers in the glow of my body.

"I'm sorry," I said, "I ask a few too many questions."

"No apology necessary. Your style of communication reminds me of Laird as a youngster. It has been some time since I've dealt with that many questions, but we'll manage. Now, in answer to your question, Geirrod and his troops have overtaken the fifth kingdom,

Valk. He has imprisoned Aesa there on an island surrounded by fire and giant piranhas. This island is in the middle of the River Kormet, and this river runs through all Roxthroe once and its surrounding kingdoms twice."

"And where's Geirrolf?"

"Geirrod used the Art of Mischief and has him permanently in the form of a gopher and locked in a bird's cage next to Laird," stated Egil and his eyelids drooped sadly.

"Where is Laird?"

"Laird, in human form, is chained by his hands to the ceiling of the tightest prison cell, and his feet are chained to the side. He hangs above a pool filled with those same giant piranhas. The saddest part is the cruelty of Geirrod. He has hung Laird's belt and hammer several feet in front of Laird's face."

With that statement, the elf touched my birthmark, and held out his hand, "Now, let us create a plan of action, a strategy, if you will."

My first instinct: I needed to get to Aesa and protect her, but I figured that "strategy" would get us caught. Quit thinking like a ten-year-old from Faulk county and start thinking like a hero, I told myself.

"Well," I said, taking the pouch back from Egil, "according to my father, Queen Linn is an expert at the Art of Mischief. Perhaps, we need to get to her first?"

"Precisely! I should explain to you that Queen Linn has instructed Elva and Aesa in that same Art of Mischief. The problem is that Geirrod's abilities in the Art of Mischief have grown as well. After Lester and Laird saved Roxsthroe from the flood, Laird exiled Geirrod to The Unknown."

Sensing my question he said, "The Unknown is the land beyond our kingdom. We call it The Unknown because it hasn't been explored since our land's infancy. While in exile and unbeknownst to Laird, Geirrod honed his skills, and he used these skills to overtake five kingdoms."

"I know," I said, putting the seeds of wheat back into the pouch, "I saw the power that he held over my dog, Frazier."

"Don't you mean Dorg, young one?"

"In my land, he is just a farm dog."

"Explain this to me, please."

"The Dorg, my farm dog, accidently fell through the rock; and he does not know how to get back through the rock."

"This Dorg is the creature that changes from a young boy to a dog to a mouse, correct?'

"No, he does not change to a boy. Geirrolf said that he changed to a mouse, and I have seen him in dog form here in Roxsthroe. But I do not think he changes to a boy."

With that statement, Egil pointed to the dark corner from which he, himself, had stepped. My golden retriever dog, Frazier, emerged from the shadows. His held his ears up, and his head tilted slightly to the left...his normal stance.

"Frazier!" I hollered. I couldn't stop myself.

Egil shushed me, but I didn't care. I ran to my dog and hugged him. I buried my face in his soft golden fur. Frazier nuzzled my ear, and I laughed. Then I felt Egil's hand on my shoulder.

"Young one, get up and step back," said Egil.

I did as I was told. Before I could speak, I watched my farm dog shift into human boy form. He appeared to be about my age, one inch taller than I; but he was skinny (like me) with dark brown eyes. His hair -- golden brown like late summer's grasses being blown by the wind -- looked like his tossled, thick dog hair. Now I was speechless.

When I regained my voice, I commanded, "Stick out your tongue!"

"What?" asked Frazier.

"I said stick out your tongue!"

The boy did as he was told, and sure enough Frazier in human form had black spots on his tongue!

"I'll be darned," I said shaking my head slowly like my mother shakes her head when I remember to put my socks away without being told.

"Master," Frazier said, "I, too, serve you. When I saw you again in the king's quarters, when you recognized me and I recognized you, that is when I felt Geirrod's hold over me lessen. Geirrod's magic, his hold over me, has been weakened with you here. Now, I am loyal to you and to Roxsthroe.

My mouth, eyes, and ears -- I opened all of my senses; but none of my senses worked. I just saw my farm dog turn into a boy. I will admit, playing with Frazier on the ranch, I'd wished he could have been a boy or that he could have spoken. How was this possible? As I asked the question, I heard the voice of the Rock, "All is possible." Huh? I thought: all is possible, even a farm dog that shifts into a human boy.

"Do I call you Frazier then?"

"Yes?"

"Does Geirrod know that you shift into human form?"

"No, only Egil and you know that."

"So, if you will, let us return to the conversation concerning our plan of attack," said Egil. "If we head to the twelfth kingdom and work our way in, then we will gain the queens as well as other loyal followers. Perhaps, by the time we reach Aesa in the fifth kingdom, we will be strong enough to overtake Geirrod."

I couldn't stop looking at Frazier, my farm dog, now in human form. I could not concentrate, so I had to look at my shoes, silently repeat what Egil had said, and then form my question.

"Why haven't the queens attacked sooner?" I asked.

"Because Queen Linn and Queen Elva await your return. They have read the Wall, and the Wall's most recent reading said, "Wait for Kvist...wait for Kvist...wait for Kvist...""

At that point we paused. Frazier and I examined our feet; Egil, the ceiling. As I thought about the next step, I fingered the pouch around my neck and thought of my dad. I wondered what he would do in this situation. In my father's story, Queen Linn ate berries to transport; perhaps if we each ate a kernel of wheat then we could transport as well. I mulled that over, like a farmer moves his chew from one cheek to his lower lip and back again. I let the thought roll through my brain like a bowling ball down the lane. Only ask, I said to myself. I swear I heard the Rock's voice, "You are good and deep soil. Those seeds of wheat will do for you what you need them to do for you."

I stood still like a white heron in a slough. Nothing moved: not my body nor my thoughts. I concentrated on my breaths in and out.

Then the thought arrived like a welcome letter from a friend. You go to the mailbox expected boring stuff like bills and junk, and then you find that letter addressed to you and written in your friend's handwriting.

I looked up at Frazier and Egil and said, "I have these seeds of wheat. The rock told me that the seeds would do for me what I needed them to do. Well, it seems that we need to get to the twelfth kingdom, so let's use the seeds."

"How?" asked Frazier.

"When my father told his tale, he said that Queen Linn would eat red berries so that she could transport. Maybe we should try eating these?" I said, but my last statement sounded more like a question.

Egil looked up at the ceiling and said, "No need to eat them. Their power works differently." But he didn't continue for several minutes. He just kept staring at the ceiling.

Finally, he stated, "Young one, after your father left, the present King Laird found me, if you will, in quite a predicament. I was surrounded by dwarfs in the forest. To save me, he cupped the pouch with both of his hands and suddenly I lifted into mid-air above the heads of the dwarfs. Then I floated over and landed behind him. As the dwarfs raced toward him, Laird took his hammer and slammed it on the ground. The ground shook like an earthquake. You should have seen those dwarfs dance," and then Egil laughed this amazing laugh. It sounded like the deep, belly laugh of a giant mixed with the child-like laughter of a toddler. His laughter made me laugh, but the thought of dwarfs dancing because of an earthquake, courtesy of King Laird, also added to my giggle. Either the dwarf image or Egil's laugh made Frazier giggle as well.

As we quieted, I said, "I think I'll give that a try. Perhaps, you'll both want to put your hands on my shoulders."

I should have been nervous, but instead my curiosity was the size of a basketball and my nervousness was the size of a baseball. When my dad told his story of Roxsthroe, he spoke of how he too had no fear when he was in Roxsthroe. He said fear came with age. Maybe people truly didn't understand fear until they were adults.

I cupped the pouch with both hands as the hands of my new friends reached for my shoulders. I closed my eyes and thought about Queen Linn and Elva. As I remembered my father's tales about them, it felt like I floated. I did not look down. I thought about how Linn saved my father's life with those berries. I thought about her courage when she lulled her husband Lain into that deep sleep of death. I thought of Elva's courage as well, how she had the presence of mind to grab the knife as they raced through the kitchen. I thought about how she had felt so badly afterward. I thought of how Linn so calmly explained that she had made the correct decision. I thought about my father's presence of mind, his quick action, when he stepped in front of Elva's knife. I floated on the knowledge of them; it felt like hours, but only minutes passed when my feet touched stone again. I opened my eyes to find two women with their backs turned toward us. They gazed off in the distance. Then I saw the sea.

I felt Frazier's hand, and then I felt Egil's hand. I spoke to the women's backs, "My father saw that same sea many years ago."

As I spoke, the women turned toward me. The older of the two, Queen Linn I presumed, said, "Yes, he did, but he saw a wall of water headed toward us. You are Kvist then."

"Yes. Yes, I am."

"Pleased to meet you. I am Queen Linn, and this is Queen Elva. Please, have a look at the sea. Tell us what you see."

I stepped up beside them and saw a calm sea. I looked to the horizon line -- a perfect line of blue. Below it, the waves were babies playing against the beach. I felt metamorphosed like a caterpillar during the most powerful part its change into the butterfly. My speechlessness turned into something else, something like prayer. This spell allowed me to see beyond the horizon line to the rising and circling sea beyond. I asked no one, "Is this a hurricane?" and no one answered. Robotically, I turned in the opposite direction of the sea, and beyond the trees I saw an army approaching. I continued in this state, going back and forth from watching the army to watching the storm approach. Then I stopped.

"Queen Linn, we have trouble on two fronts!"

"He sees!" Elva said slightly breathless. "Linn, is it the power of the rock?"

"I believe so. Correct, young one, but only one of these fronts is trouble. The sea only. The gathering army -- our allies -- is for me, for my family, and for life in Roxthroe as we have come to know it," Linn said calmly. My dad had described her calm voice, but beings as he is a man of few words, his description did not do it justice.

"An army gathers against Geirrod?" asked Egil, "without being summoned?"

"Yes," answered Linn, "and I can't tell for sure if it is the power of the wall. Like I said, we shall have to wait and see."

"What can be done about this storm?" I asked.

"Young one, the wall said that you could dissolve the storm," said Linn calmly. I couldn't put my finger on what her voice sounded like. It reminded me of a slight South Dakota breeze, the kind welcomed on a hot day.

"Excuse me?" I asked.

"I can say only what the Wall has told me. First the Wall said, 'Wait for Kvist...wait for Kvist...wait for Kvist...' One week later, the Wall said, 'Kvist will walk on water to calm the storm...'"

"Are you sure that you read that right?" I asked. "No offense, Queen Linn. I can swim just fine, but last time I checked, I could not walk on water. Are we sure we believe the wall?"

"Yes," replied Linn, Elva, Egil, and Frazier simultaneously.

"Yes," came a chorus of voices to the right and to the left.

I looked to the right and saw women dressed like nuns, and I looked to the left and saw men dressed like priests.

The resounding roomful of "yeses" stunned me. It felt good, an affirmation, like when your teacher tells you that you are really good at math when you have always thought that you were better at reading. So I turned back toward the sea. I cupped my hands and silently stated this: I will walk on water. Show me how. As I repeated these statements, I watched the sea. The horizon line changed. With each silent word, it shifted further into haze. The haze changed to wind and proceeded toward me. I felt like I was on top of the hay bales -- poised and ready to jump across the 20 foot high void -- to the next stack. Anxiety started to crawl onto my toes and up my legs, but I pushed it back.

Linn interrupted my thoughts. Her voice waved through my thoughts. She said, "We will give you time. We will be just down the hallway when you finish. Though you will be alone, please know that we will be down the hallway waiting for you in this church, this fortress, this sanctuary. You will succeed, Kvist."

For a moment, my faith wavered, and again I wondered if the wall had really seen this happening.

She heard my thought, "No, the wall cannot see; the wall can only predict, can only give opportunity. The rest lies within the person."

I am not big on prayer --I pray in my own church and at bedtime, but I just never really needed to pray outside of the church; however, since I was in church I decided it wouldn't hurt. My mom prayed lots though. My mom, who rarely misses church, says that we should thank Him and then ask Him. So, I gave it try: "Lord, thank You for my blessings: my family, our farm, and my friends, old and new. Give me strength, the strength that you gave my father. Give me the power to succeed. Help me to save this church and these people from the winds upon the sea."

I heard the Rock's voice, "Those who are deep and good soil can do all things. Go, young one. Float."

With that, I cupped my hands under the pouch, and I floated. This time I kept my eyes open. It felt like the college football national championship; the Huskers were winning, and I wanted my eyes wide open so that I didn't miss one play.

As I approached the storm, I grew, and not just a little either. I watched each hand become the size of an apple tree and each foot become the size of a flatbed full of square bales. I thought, I am the size of a Tyrannosaurus Rex. I watched the sea below my feet; slowly it turned from calm to stormy, like water coming to a boil. Soon I floated down to the surface, and my feet landed. As I walked toward the storm, I thought of Peter in the Bible. I heard a voice speak, "Come." I walked toward the voice thinking of the story of Peter. I could learn from him. He walked on water but sank because he wavered. Maybe if he'd been but a boy instead of a man, I thought. I knew that the wind made him afraid. I listened to the whipping wind; it blew and then it snapped like 100 whips. The storm grew, but fear was nowhere near me.

"I love storms!" I said, but I wasn't sure to whom I spoke; perhaps I spoke to fear itself. As I continued walking toward the voice, I thought of the time that my family piled into the truck one early evening and drove to the top of a nearby hill to watch a thunderstorm; the thunder and lightning and rain headed toward us, but we were not afraid. We were together! First, the clouds appeared the darkest blue, navy-blue almost. Bank upon bank of navy-blueness approached us. Evening approached as well in oranges and yellows and grays. From the clouds came lightning bolts, flashes of light so fast that, for a moment, we were blinded, but we regained our vision as we waited for the next bolt. The thunder was a cradle rocking us, and it lulled us before, during, and after the storm. When the rain arrived, the drops saturated the ground and left a haze at the base of our hill. We watched for one solid hour. As it approached, I felt calmness. The rain hypnotized: so much so that I fell asleep. When I woke up, my father carried me through the door and into my bedroom. My mom fluffed my hair saying, "Sleepy head, the storm did you in?" I fell asleep that night with my mom kneeling beside me, running her fingers through my hair.

With that memory, my body increased in size again. Now my hands were the size of an oak tree, and my feet were the size of two full flat beds of square bales. I looked at the hurricane; now I was larger than this storm.

What could I do to dissolve a hurricane? If I jumped into the middle of it, then smaller storms would be pushed out in all directions. That could be bad because these small storms could increase in size as they headed toward the coast.

What could I do to dissolve this storm? The answer led my feet and my open arms toward the hurricane. I enclosed the storm in my arms, and I squeezed with all my might. My arms, in a bear hug, squeezed the life out of this storm. As I squeezed, the circular storm lost some strength and some weight; it went from a plump hurricane to a skinny tornado. With all my might, I pushed that tornado back out to sea. It rose toward the horizon line. When it reached the line, it collapsed like a tower of toy blocks.

I breathed in and out. Then I walked back toward shore. At the shoreline, I shrunk back to the size of a boy.

Chapter 15

On the shore, I had to stop to catch my breath. I waited for my heart and breathing rates to return to normal.

I looked up at the sky and spoke, "I feel like I hit a grand slam during the final game of the World Series. Awesome!" I'd felt it before, but beating – outmaneuvering wrestling opponents, one of my favorite hobbies – was nothing compared to beating, outmaneuvering a hurricane! Today, my favorite hobby had been replaced!

"Did I really just do that?" I asked the sky again. In disbelief, I looked out to the sea in its new calmness. The height of the ocean amazed me. I marveled at how the ocean rose above me, above the beach. Waves rode into the shoreline, but my eyes went up to the horizon line. The blue stretched upwards, and this upward stretch made me feel small, as if I stood next to the rock in his bowl in our pasture.

I turned away to gain my bearing and examined the fortification before me. This cliff protruded, and, on both sides, forests of trees cuddled up next to it. The fort, church – a castle really – had been built into the cliff in such a way that it blended in with the clay-colored rock. In fact, at first glance I thought I had landed on a different beach. This fort was camouflaged like a deer within a thicket.

I located the stairs that zig-zagged up the side, and I climbed. Frazier met me on the stairs and exclaimed, "Amazing! The hurricane was a shrimp compared to you. You were bigger than our biggest giant; you were bigger than Geirrolf. In fact, I believe that you were larger than Laird when he puts on his belt. Amazing!"

As we entered the room, Queen Linn approached me first, "Your greatness of character and your presence of mind have restored my faith. You are Lester's son."

The room echoed Frazier's initial reaction. I heard the word *amazing* countless times.

As the excitement started to quiet, I looked at Egil and said, "What next?'

And he, being a slight know-it-all took me seriously. In a matter-of-fact voice, he said, "No time to waste. In order for our army to be complete, we will need the strength of Aesa and her Art of Mischief. Her power, coupled with the power of Linn and Elva, will be necessary for us to defeat Geirrod and his forces."

As he spoke, he looked toward Elva's worried face. I walked up next to her, and she took my hand. I said to her, "I know of you through my father. He said that you loved adventure. I need to tell you something. I met Aesa. I watched her in action. I think she follows in your footsteps. So creative and – well, honestly – she has no fear."

Elva's worried expression turned into a tiny smile, "You, young one, are a man of fine words. You are wise beyond your years."

"Thank you, ma'am," I said staring at Egil. "Some might say that I enjoy going off on a – what did you call it Egil? – that's right...a tangent."

Egil laughed loudly.

Through his laughter, Elva asked, "Would your father be Lester Louis Hansen?"

"Yes, ma'am, and when I told him that Aesa had green apple eyes, he said that Laird must have married you."

"And Lester married as well. Your mother is a very blessed woman."

"Thank you, ma'am, as are you. Aesa is a really smart and brave and...well...her eyes look like green apples, like I said before."

Both Linn and Elva smiled as I stumbled over my words like one stumbled over dirt clods in a plowed field. Once again, redness overtook my face.

Egil saved me. I had to give him credit. He might be a bit arrogant, but he did save me from my embarrassing predicament. Egil continiued with the strategizing, "I think our wisest plan of attack should involve as few people as possible. If we keep our troops secret, then we will have the upper hand. A surprise attack, if you will."

"Egil, a stop at the Wall and then to Valk and the Island of Fire. I will be going with you to read the wall," Elva spoke with a calmness so similar to Linn. I wondered if reading the wall connected with the Art of Mischief. I wondered, but I did not ask.

"Your highness, we will need you to read the wall, but we cannot risk your safety," Egil spoke but his eyes were averted.

"My safety is of less value than Kvist's safety. That being said, I shall read the wall for you and then depart back to Loxsney, the twelfth kingdom, to await your return. When you return, you will have my daughter."

Linn held out eight berries, giving two to Elva, Egil, Frazier, and me. I knew without being told what these berries would do, for my father told me about using berries to transport. Linn spoke, "Remember, these berries work only when one of us is with you. Elva will get you to the Wall. Then you must get to Valk on your own accord. Once you have retrieved Aesa, she can transport you back."

She handed me one more berry. Closing my hand around it, she said, "An extra just in case Aesa does not have a berry available within the circle of fire. Good luck, young one."

We four looked at each other, plopped a berry in our mouths, and disappeared.

Chapter 16

I felt about the wall as I had felt about the sea: full of awe. The wall looked like the gate to a pen of trees. Let me explain. A circle of twenty trees appeared in a clearing in the middle of a forest. Each huge tree in the circle had ten feet between itself and the next tree. The two biggest of the twenty trees "held" the wall and reigned with majestic crowns of leaves which stretched ten feet above the other trees, and the wall was between those two trees. Large rocks, field stones stacked one upon another, made up the wall. Some of the rocks sat nervously and looked like they might topple at any moment.

I leaned over to Frazier and whispered, "It looks like someone took one of our rock piles and turned it into a wall. How many stones do you think?"

"Beats me," he whispered back.

Questions pummeled my brain like punches from a prize fighter. How had the wall been built? Who built it? When was it built? Were its predictions ever wrong? Had a rock ever fallen off or out of the wall? If it was a gate, then, I wondered, had it ever been opened?

Egil spoke first, "As a guardian elf, I can sense your questions and concerns. The wall has been around since the beginning of time. No one knows from where it came. Legends abound. I side with those who believe that it just appeared, like someone striking a match to produce a flame, if you will. The wall's predictions have never been wrong. As a gate, it has never been used, but what an interesting inquiry, young one."

"On the ranch, we operate by gates," I looked at Elva and asked, "Did you receive training in reading the wall?"

"Some can be trained; for me it came with time and no training. I first saw the wall with Laird and Geirrolf when I was a young girl. Has your father told you that story?" she asked and I nodded as a means of letting her know to continue.

"At that time, I saw no messages, but each trip I tried to watch and learn. I'd make my trips to the wall with Geirrolf because he read very well. I learned intuitively."

I interrupted, "What's intuitively mean?"

"Animals have instincts, correct?" asked Elva.

"Yes."

"My ability to read the wall was something I just knew like an instinct. I just knew how to read it, like someone who doesn't need much training. I just had a gift."

"Oh," I said.

"On my fifth trip to the wall, I could read with the same speed as Geirrolf. This impressed Geirrolf; and he said, 'It took me an entire childhood to learn to read the wall. What did you do that I didn't do?' I said, 'I concentrated on just one rock,' and then he said, 'Guess I'll have to try that.' Now, I can read with the same speed that horses can run."

"Enough questions, Young One. Now, step back, young one, so that Elva can have some space," commanded Egil. He sensed my pyramid of questions.

Frazier and I stepped back, and I asked Elva, "Can I help? Do you think I could read the wall?"

"Yes, you can help and you can try. The closer you can get to your own heart and soul, the more power is generated; and that power helps you read. Think of something -- maybe a song from childhood -- that might help you focus."

We watched in silence, an introverted prayer session. As I watched the stones shift, I thought of a song my mom would sing to me when I was younger. She'd sing: "Down in the valley, the valley so low. Hang your head over. Hear the wind blow. Hear the wind blow, dear. Hear the wind blow. Hang your head over. Hear the wind blow."

I repeated that verse over and over. It felt like jumping into a cool pool of water on a hot day. Between each verse, I looked up at Elva and watched. She pressed her hands together, but she did not fold her fingers. The fingers of her left hand touched the fingers of her right hand. She held her hands just beneath her head, and her head was slightly bowed. Was she even looking at the wall, I wondered? I could feel my mind straying from the song because I kept looking up at Elva again. I tried again. I closed my eyes and thought of my mom and how she would sing it to me every day and more than once on the days when I felt down. I said the song over again in my head, but I heard the smallest creak; and I looked up again. This time I watched the wall. I remembered that my father had said, according to Geirrolf's story, that when the rocks shifted they creaked like the joints of an arthritic old man. As I watched the rocks shift, I heard very few creaks. I wondered why the rocks didn't creak as much. Maybe they'd been read so often that the rocks had been ground away. Again, I realized that my mind was wandering away from the song. I started up the second verse of "Down in the Valley" one more time.

Elva spoke as I neared the end of the second verse, "I have it, and I understand it."

"Thank goodness," stated Egil flatly, "because our young one's head is very full of questions. His questions interrupted his thoughts and mine."

"So sorry, Egil," I said, "I really have trouble focusing when my brain fills with questions, and my brain fills with questions quite often."

"That is an understatement!" exclaimed Egil, "Queen Elva, please tell us what you've read."

"The wall says this, 'The fire's ring can be penetrated by the one called Frazier, but first we must find the shape-shifter named Ernst.'

"We need Ernst then," said Egil in a matter-of-fact way.

"I am the only one who can penetrate the fire?" questioned Frazier, "but how can that be since I've been aiding Geirrod. What if my magic doesn't work? What if I kill Aesa?"

I looked at Frazier and said, "The wall has never been wrong. Remember that. It said I'd walk on water, and I did."

"Our first step will be to find Ernst," said Egil.

"Where might we find Ernst?" I asked Egil.

"You and your questions. Who answers them in Hansenville?" asked Egil.

"My father and my mother mostly. Sometimes my older brothers. My sister, rarely," I stated as I rolled my eyes.

"Your poor kin. I think I'd have to start falsifying the truth with you," stated Egil.

"What does falsifying mean?"

"Oh my...another question then. Falsifying means lying, if you will. Now hold those questions please," stated Egil, and I remained silent.

In silence, I kept my hand on Frazier's shoulder, and I kept catching his eye. His nervousness reverberated against my hand, but I kept my hand there in reassurance.

Egil continued, "Ernst -- an elf like me -- probably lives in the sixth kingdom; and if I know Ernst, he hasn't moved too far. This is good because the sixth kingdom is on our way to Aesa's prison on the Island of Fire in Valk. Off to the sixth kingdom, Alfaland, then."

I watched Frazier carefully; he seemed better, not quite like the scared puppy of a few minutes ago.

Egil read my mind, "You seem better, Frazier, calmer, if you will."

Frazier said, "One must believe. I guess that I just have to believe in myself."

"Then let us depart. Finding Ernst could be tricky as he is a bit of a recluse."

I began to ask what "recluse" meant, but Egil stopped me with his hand, "A recluse is someone who lives in seclusion for meditative purposes, who lives alone to pray, if you will. The good news is that I visited him quite often as a youth; but the bad news is that the last time I visited him, he had become a curmudgeon," he looked directly at me and said, "A curmudgeon is a grumpy old man."

I looked directly back, shaking my head, and said, "I wasn't going to ask that question," but Egil knew better. He knew that the question was coming his way with the speed of a fastball.

Elva giggled. She sounded like my mom, and, for a moment, I lost myself in the feeling of home.

Egil turned to Elva and said, "Your Highness, we leave you here. We bid you safe passage back to the twelfth kingdom."

We watched her put a berry in her mouth and disappear into thin air. Then we looked around at each other, chewed our second berry, and we too disappeared.

Chapter 17

We landed in the crook of a tree, a gigantic oak tree. An amazing tree house grew out of the crook. It looked exactly like an A-frame house, a perfect triangle for a top and its bottom had been set into the crook of the tree. A darker brown door with a great window above it and two windows on each side welcomed us to the house. We stepped onto the mat in front of the door.

"What does 'Velkomen' mean?" I asked.

"It means 'Welcome,'" replied Egil.

"Egil, he is not a recluse. He welcomes you, see," I said and pointed at the mat.

As Egil knocked, he said, "Please note the rugged condition of the mat; it is older than I. By the way, do not look behind you."

If someone tells a curious person like me that he should not look behind him, then more than likely that curious person tends to look behind him. Thank goodness that I did look behind me. Although the height dizzied me, the view was fascinating. Below us grew a forest of trees; to the sides of us, leaves; so many that we couldn't see past the crook of the tree; and above, leaves, although we could see tiny scraps of blue sky.

The dark brown door opened, and a definite curmudgeon stood before us. I had called Egil a gnome, but this gentleman resembled one even more than Egil. An oversized gnome stood before us, except really he was a shrunken, grumpy, old elf. His beard and hair were white; his coat was blue; his pants and boots were brown; and his elf hat was red. The only difference between this elf and what I imagined a gnome to look like was the size. This creature was not the size of a human's thumb. This creature was the exact replica of the gnome that sat in my Grandma Malinda's garden, but this was an elf. He was several inches smaller than Egil, but his voice boomed like a grain truck rattling down a gravel road.

"I knew that you were coming for me," stated Ernst.

"How?" I couldn't help myself.

"Forgive the young one, for he is full of questions. I have not answered this many questions since Laird was a boy," stated Egil shaking his head. "I have not taken the time to explain to him that you, like many skilled in the Art of Mischief, can read minds and see the future."

As Egil spoke, Ernst began to laugh, and his belly-laugh made me feel comfortable enough to say, "I apologize, Ernst. I should learn to keep my questions to myself."

My apology made Ernst laugh even harder, and this made Egil laugh as well. To laugh did not seem to be Egil's style. He seemed rather serious, but apparently Ernst brought out a different side of him. Ernst even winked at me as he laughed.

"Indeed," said Ernst through guffaws of laughter, "he is quite a bit like a young Laird, isn't he?"

His laughter ended like a lightning strike, and he spoke without laughter, "Do his powers compare to Laird's?"

"He holds the pouch, and that, coupled with an immense amount of faith, makes him rather formidable," stated Egil, and knowing that his word choice would spawn a question from me, he continued by saying, "Formidable means that you are powerful enough to protect yourself in a world of giants, if you will."

"Oh," I said, and for once, I couldn't think of anything else to say.

Egil continued, "Ernst, please put our disagreements behind us. Our country's freedom is at stake. Please, tell me what you've seen."

With that, Ernst stepped back and swept his arm in front of us saying, "Velkomen."

I entered first, but I stopped like a car at a stop sign. I was in awe of my surroundings. Frazier was in awe too, and I know this because he walked right into me. I turned toward him, and, for just one moment we stared at each other wide-eyed like two kids at an amusement park; then we couldn't help ourselves and our eyes scanned everything like when you first walk into a giant toy store. Everywhere I looked in Ernst's house, a miracle could be found. I stepped off to the right, thinking I'd look out that window. Instead of being clear glass and rectangular, as it had appeared on the outside of the house, this window was stained glass and shaped like an oak leaf. Without speaking, I walked back outside to the floor mat and turned toward that window. It looked clear, and, here is the crazy part, I could see Ernst, Egil, and Frazier inside the house. I walked back inside and stood in front of the window again. The light filtered through the stained glass, and colored lights searched the room like beacons. The color red landed on my hand. I lifted my hand, and it passed through a myriad of colors; each color seemed to scrutinize my hand for an explanation. I stepped back and out of the colored light. I put my right arm across my chest. I balanced my left elbow on my right arm, and I put my left fist under my chin. Once again, I looked like that famous statue, "The Thinker," but I stood.

Ernst had taken a seat in a leather chair, and from the chair he spoke to me, "Young one, what is your name?"

"Kip John Hansen. I am named after my grandfather," I said, not mentioning the soap opera star story this time.

"And after a soap opera star," said Ernst back to me.

The stare I gave him was my question.

"I read minds, remember. How did it feel to stand in the light of my window?" he asked.

"Strange," I said, "as if the colors asked me questions."

"Not the colors," he said, "but the tree. My tree is trying to get to know you. I shall explain later." He shifted in his chair and spoke to Egil.

"The escape of Aesa from the Island of Fire will occur. I see her and, well, that boy right there," he said and pointed at Frazier, "escaping the flames on the horse who can withstand the heat, and that steed is I."

"But you cannot shift to a horse? I thought you could shift only to a vole?"

"And I still can, but I've trained myself to shift to a steed."

Egil stood from his chair opposite Ernst, folded his arms roughly, and asked, "How? How can that be?"

"My study of the Art of Mischief goes well, to say the least. With intense meditation and the aid of the cone flower, I am able to change to stallion form. Several months ago, the first vision came: I saw myself as an elf and then a vole and then a huge, black stallion. Its shiny coat protects it from heat. Because this stallion kept appearing in my visions and kept appearing as another version of me, I decided to try to will myself to become it. It worked, but you must believe. I will not shift here or my stallion self will wreak havoc on my home."

He looked at me and said, "Wreak havoc means destroy. As you can imagine, a strong steed could topple this small A-frame. And my home is just as I like it. If it were destroyed, then I would have to start over."

I liked Ernst. It seemed like he welcomed my questions, so I asked him, "Did you see that I have a part in the rescue of Aesa?"

As he spoke, he shook his head from side to side, "Young one, you must stay away from this adventure. Your presence there could cause grave danger for Aesa. Your calling was calming the storm, and later you will free Laird and Geirrolf. For this journey, you must stay on the other shore, no matter what."

I felt my eyes lower; I searched my shoes for an explanation of the feeling that came over me. My shoes revealed nothing but dirt, the dirt of home mixed with the dirt of this world. In my examination of my dirt, I realized that I felt disappointed because I wanted to save Aesa. I wanted to be her hero, but what good would that do? I had dirt from both worlds on my shoes. In my heart, I knew that the dirt of my world was more important. True, I said to myself, hunting gophers was never as exciting as a trip to Roxsthroe, but even if my world tended to be a bit boring, it was my world; it held my family and my farm. I would have to be the hero of my own world. Then I remembered that Ernst could read my thoughts.

He said nothing, just smiled and nodded at me, "Why don't you take a look around."

As I started to explore, I left my disappointment behind for too many amazing sights awaited me. Ernst's house was a true A-frame with vaulted ceilings and a loft. Just in front of the loft was the chandelier, the lighting unit for the whole house. I stepped up next to Frazier, whose eyes were fixed on that chandelier. Made of antlers, it was suspended from nothing. It had no strings or cables attached to it, yet it lit the entire house.

Frazier elbowed me but then said, "Sorry," as he realized that I stared at it too. Once he had elbowed me, I shifted my eyes, for other wonders and marvels revealed themselves. Inside the front door, each wall had a magic stained glass window.

"What direction?" I asked pointing toward the front wall.

"North," said Frazier, "toward the sea."

The east and west walls stretched toward the loft. A huge book shelf lined each of the side walls. As I approached the bookshelf on the west wall, the shelf shrunk away from me leaving wall space. I looked around and both book shelves had shrunk back into the walls. Now, the walls matched the wooden floors and the ceiling, all made of the most beautiful wood, unstained oak, one shade from the color white, like harvested wheat. I ran my hands along the walls. I couldn't resist. The walls were so smooth and warm, life-like, as if the walls had a soul. The furniture was wooden and of that same smooth, unstained oak, and because Frazier and I were but boys, we could still fit into the furniture. I took a seat in a chair across from Ernst. There I noticed four stacks of books underneath the other window. These books had not been in the shelves. I examined the stacks of books, which looked like a city scape with differing heights of skyscrapers. I couldn't help but wonder how an elf could reach the highest book if he wanted to read it?

"Why aren't those books in your bookcase?" I asked.

"These books rarely find the book shelf. These books are my most important ones," Ernst said, and clapped his hands.

We watched as a book pulled itself from the fourth stack of the second row. It floated toward us and dropped itself at my feet. I reached for it and read its title, *The History of Roxsthroe*, by Ernst Johnson.

"Amazing," I said.

"What? The fact that the book floated or the fact that I wrote a book?" Ernst asked.

"Both," I answered.

From my seat, I noticed the table that took up most of this great room. It was the only bit of furniture made without one bit of wood. I stepped up to it, and ran my fingers along the back of one of the chairs. It felt like cement or a really thick, solid plaster, and it looked like an elongated daisy with stunted petals! The smooth table top was in the shape of an oval, and the chairs were attached to the table much like petals, short, squat daisy petals. Each petal had a leather cushion, and each seat was enclosed from the back of the chair to the bottom of the chair, and from the right side of the chair to the left. I could not get into the chair. As I stood there in fascination, the left chair opened to let me in. I stepped up and sat down at the table.

"Amazing," I spoke without thinking.

"Out you come, young one," said Egil, "we haven't time for your curiosity. Come. We have some miles to go to get us to the island."

Though fascinated and focused on the marvels of Ernst's home, we followed him. We walked past the stairs that led to the loft. Beneath the loft, we found the kitchen and eating area. A large island of a counter rested within the kitchen area. Pots, pans, and strange utensils hung above the island, suspended by the same magic as the antler chandelier. The eating area appeared to be quite simple: a large oak table and 12 simple oak chairs. I walked over to it and ran my hand across it, half-expecting it to disappear like the bookshelves. Nothing happened except that once again the wood felt alive and warm.

It struck me then. This tree lives, which I knew from its outward appearance. It had green leaves, for goodness sakes, but this tree lived in a different sort of way from other normal trees. It grew within Ernst's house. It powered Ernst's house. Like a human with a heart and blood vessels and a soul and a personality all its own. I shrugged my shoulders thinking maybe all trees were like this. Alive within! But we humans just don't take the time to notice.

Ernst stopped, and with his back still turned to me, said, "The table is magical too, you know."

"How?" I asked.

"It sets itself, clears itself, and even does the dishes!"

"Are you married?"

"No. Why?" he said giggling. I think he saw where I was going with this.

"With that kind of magic," I said, "I would think you'd be irresistible. A magical table probably works better than underarm deodorant and cologne!"

At the back wall between the kitchen and the dining area, Ernst stopped abruptly. He paused, and then the most wonderful laughter erupted from his body. Egil joined him.

As they laughed, I leaned over to Frazier and said, "He's not that crotchety."

With that statement, Ernst laughed even harder. As Ernst and Egil tried to stop laughing, I looked back at the oak table and chair. They were the same color as the walls, that simple, unstained, elegant yet plain oak color. A tablecloth that looked like oak leaves weaved together covered the table. Each chair had a backrest and pad made of that same leave fabric.

I wondered how that magic worked. All the walls, all the floors and ceilings, and all the furniture were the same beautiful color. All were alive from the tree. I was perplexed but I did not ask any questions.

How could a table and chairs set themselves, clear themselves, and then, on top of all that, do their own dishes? About to turn away, I saw the far chair move out of the corner of my eye. I looked back quickly and watched the table become a slightly overweight elf woman, and the chairs transformed into elves as well. Without taking notice of us, they marched into the kitchen area and set to work grabbing plates and cups from the cupboard and silverware from the drawers. Before my eyes, the table and chairs took their places in the dining area; and -- POOF -- the table was set, and the chairs were all pushed in next to the table!

"That is crazy!" I said. "Ernst, I really must learn more about all of this! You cannot expect a curious kid like me to go back to my regular routine on the ranch!"

Once again, I made the elves laugh. Ernst laughed so hard that he had to bend over. As he righted himself, he placed his hand on Egil's arm as if to steady himself. Then he took a deep breath in and pushed it out as if he smoked a pipe and made a smoke ring. Ernst and Egil gained control and stopped their laughter. The stoppage of laughter made me think that maybe Ernst might be ready to take me seriously about learning more.

Finally, Ernst replied, "We shall see what can be arranged after we've saved the kingdom and your ranch."

As he said this he rested his palm upon the wall. A door appeared. Before we knew it, we were led into a small closet.

Frazier said, "What are we doing in a closet?"

Ernst said, "'Tis no closet; 'tis an elevator. It will take us to the ground floor."

"Is it within the tree?" I asked.

"Yes, this tree is my oldest friend. Each time you touched something in my house, she touched you. Could you feel her?"

"I think so," I said. "The walls were so warm when I touched them."

"You could say that the warmth comes from her life. As you touched her, you allowed her into your soul."

"Can she read my thoughts like you and Egil?

"She read you like a book! Keep in mind always that if we provide for the trees, then they will provide for us. I provide for her and she for me."

"Is she like a sister?" I asked.

"Similar, but she is motherly as well. She cares for me when I am ill."

"Oh?" I said looking toward Ernst.

Egil answered instead, "Trees have therapeutic skills. They feel our pain, and they can heal us through our senses."

I furrowed my brow in confusion. First, I didn't understand Egil's answer, and second, I wanted Ernst to continue explaining. Then I frowned because I knew that both men were reading my mind. Ernst grinned, and Egil, as usual, ignored my thought, and continued speaking.

"When we are sad, they offer us care with their beauty and their smell and their noises. Have you ever felt better because of a tree?" Egil asked me.

"Maybe. But I didn't know it."

"Trees can diagnose pain and repair it, if you will," stated Egil.

"How?" I asked, hoping I had asked before Frazier because I hoped Frazier was as inquisitive as I.

Ernst interrupted, "I have a story that might illustrate this story for you. Once, when I gathered herbs for my potions, I tripped over a tree trunk, sprained my ankle, and scraped up my knee and hand. I limped home, put my foot up, and iced my scrapes. Within 20 minutes, I felt my tree enveloping me. All of my senses reached a heightened state. I saw her, felt her, smelled her more clearly. As I allowed myself to sink into her, she began to heal me. Finally, when I looked down at my scrapes, some of the lacerations were fully healed, and some were healing as I watched. She heals my mental states too sometimes: if I am sad, she cheers me up; if I am confused, she gives me suggestions; if I am mad, she calms me down. The power of a tree is very large."

"Oh," I said as we exited the tree at its base. I must admit that as I looked back at her leaves, the ones that were closest to me rustled. Perhaps she says goodbye, too, I thought.

In that instant, Ernst shifted from an elf to a black stallion. Off we rode.

Upon the black stallion rode two blonde boys and an elf. Frazier rode up front; Egil was in the middle; and I rode at the back. My ride on the back of that stallion through the thickest forest I've ever encountered was bumpy and uncomfortable like all of my school bus rides, but the pouch full of wheat bounced up to my chin reminding me of my purpose. I could do nothing for Aesa but watch her rescue. For a moment, I thought of her green apple eyes. I was excited to see her again, but what would she think of me since I was to do nothing to aide her. Lost in the thought of her made the ride go very quickly.

Chapter 18

When we reached the banks of the Kormet River, Ernst shifted back to elf form, dropping us all on our bottoms just like when a friend jumps off the teeter totter and leaves you to drop to the dirt.

As I stood, I examined the island; indeed fire -- composed of very large flames -- surrounded it. The flames reached high, but we could see the island because it formed a hill. At the top of the hill sat a glass case, where a figure lay. Her hands were folded on her mid-section. She reminded me of the one dead body that I'd seen in my life. When my great-uncle passed away, I went to the funeral not knowing what to expect. I saw my first open-casket and my first dead body! Uncle Ollie's eyes were closed and his hands were folded just like Aesa's. A wave of fear rolled over me as I thought of her dead body. To shake that feeling, I thought about the greenness of her eyes, so like the green in the leaves of the forest as the light hits them from up above. I'd seen that green as we rode on the stallion's back. That greenness would live. She would live.

"There's Aesa!" I exclaimed.

"Yes, I see her too," said Egil, and then he turned to us and asked, "First, we need to deal with those piranhas?" In silence, we watched the piranhas jump out of the water. One jumped out of the water and toward us; his eyes looked possessed, and his under-bite and teeth reminded me of the movie *Jaws*. I'd seen that movie just recently, and I couldn't sleep or even consider going swimming in the dug-out for several days after that. As I watched them jump in the Kormet River, I tried to count. I estimated there to be two dozen circling that island. Each piranha appeared to be about the size of a pony, and that thought made me recall my father's tale of how he and Laird had ridden the giant piranhas and how he had nearly drowned. As I watched the patterns, I wondered how my dad, who is afraid of only one earthly element and that is water, who never learned to swim, had decided that riding a giant piranha like a bucking horse would be a good idea?

The silence stretched like the pause before a teacher hands back a really tough spelling test. Ernst had said that I couldn't help save Aesa, but maybe I could think of a plan for those giant piranhas.

Ernst had said that I had to stay on the shorelines. Could I enter the water around the island? Maybe Ernst meant only on the island.

I thought of going with my grandpa and grandma on fishing trips. I saw us sitting in the boat, Grandpa Jack doing all the work while Grandma Malinda and I leaned back with our faces to the sun. We'd drag our hands through the cool water. Grandpa Jack would scold us for our laziness and then chuckle at us all in the same breath; we'd ignore his comments. Maybe I should go fishing, I thought to myself.

"You said that I couldn't help save Aesa." I said. "I won't be able to go onto the island, but could I help from the shoreline?"

"My first vision showed you on the island, and that vision showed Aesa's botched escape. My second vision showed you on the shoreline, and that vision showed Frazier and Aesa riding on the black stallion. Perhaps, yes, you could help from the shoreline. Do you have an idea?" Ernst finished and gave me an inquisitive look.

I cupped the pouch and said, "This gives me what I need. What we need right now is to go fishing. We need to lure those giant piranhas away from that island, and then we need to catch them. What we need are some fishing poles, a dozen cuts of roast beef, and one giant, namely me. Should I proceed?"

Ernst and Egil stared at each other. I could tell that they were having a silent conversation because of their facial expressions. I resisted the urge to ask any questions or make any more statements.

Finally, Egil said, "We agree to give your idea a try. Ernst did not have a vision of the piranhas, so we can assume that your assistance will be fine."

I wasted no time. I looked down at my pouch and cupped it like I was drinking water from the outdoor spicket. I concentrated with all my might on making giant fishing poles appear. I needed enough beef to catch all of them, and I needed to be transformed into a giant like when I fought the hurricane.

To concentrate without allowing questions into my brain, I kept picturing what I needed, and I closed my eyes and concentrated on those memories of fishing with my grandparents. Then I thought of grandpa's tackle box and fishing poles leaning up against the wall of his garage. Finally, I returned to what I needed: giant fishing poles, beef roasts, and growth.

First, I felt myself growing; then, I watched the ground and felt like Jack must have felt when the beanstalk took him through the clouds, only I stopped short of the clouds. I reached down, grabbed a fishing pole and a hunk of beef. I could not help but wonder if Roxsthroe raised cattle. Save it, I said to myself, and I stopped my wandering brain, stored that question, and cast my line out toward the island. It took only a moment for those blood-thirsty piranhas to smell and taste the scrumptiousness of beef. My bobber alerted me, but I remained calm and slow with that first fish. I wanted them all to get a tiny taste of the goodness of beef. I could feel my line jerking, and I hoped the others had gotten a taste. Then, I reeled that piranha in with the ferociousness of an avid fisherman catching a trophy walleye. The huge piranha felt like a small perch in my gigantic hands. I picked him up by the tail end, ripped him from my hook, and slammed him against the nearest tree, killing him instantly. I did that with each of the 28 fish -- two more than I thought -- that circled Aesa on that island. I knew that I had them all because, in my giant form, I could peer over the river and see down to the bottom; and I could see all around the island; in fact, I could probably have touched the island, but I didn't because I knew that would cause Aesa undue pain.

Then, with my work finished, I calmly shifted back into boy form like a exhausted farmer during harvest falls into his recliner to wait for supper, a shower, and bed.

Frazier stared at me and said, "Ernst, I am the wrong boy for this job. I know what you saw in your vision, but I think I am all wrong for this job. Send Kvist instead."

I stared back at Frazier and said, "Frazier, this is your destiny. True, for a short time, your calling was to be our farm dog. Remember that you survived the abuse of that puppy mill. You did. Remember how we saved you when the pound had decided that you'd have to be put to sleep. Remember how my dad called my mom and said, 'Come to town. There's a dog.' Our destiny was to save you, but you saved me instead. You gave me companionship; you gave companionship to a bored farm kid who had run out of adventures and bb's for his gun.

Sometimes, I even wished that you could talk. Don't you understand destiny? This is yours. The fact that I've found you and that I can finally talk to you is amazing, a miracle! Do you not see that now you must save Aesa like you saved me? Think of it in this simple circular way: I saved you; you saved me; and now we save Aesa. I did the fishing, but now you must get her off the island. You are Aesa's only hope, and we need her to continue with our plan. Please, Frazier, have faith in your abilities."

I spoke to Frazier's lowered head. In the pause that followed, he raised his head and looked me in the eye.

"You are my best friend too," Frazier said. Then he looked at Ernst and said, "It is time. Shift to your vole form and ride on my head across to the island."

Then he shifted to dog form. He slid his head under my hand, and I scratched under his furry chin, just like old times.

Egil and I watched from the shoreline. Frazier's dog head, with Ernst the vole atop, bobbed, and his tail swished through the water as he swam to the island. As they reached the edge of the island, I sighed relief.

Egil said, "You killed them all, young one. All of those fish are dead, and not one of them escaped. What character and intelligence you have displayed again! I am proud of you."

Pretty sure that Egil did not show pride toward others very often, I smiled a very large grin, so large that all my teeth, even my back molars, showed.

Flames engulfed the outer edge of the island, all except one tiny little edge. I wondered why.

Reading my mind and knowing my question, Ernst said, "One could suppose that Geirrod cast his spell from that particular spot."

"Oh, that makes sense," I said as we continued to watch.

Frazier and Ernst headed for this tiny piece of land. Frazier stepped out of the water, allowed Ernst to get down, and then Frazier shook his golden fur until it dried. Frazier shifted to mouse, and Ernst shifted from vole to elf. From his belt pouch, he took a vial. As he poured it over the fire, a small hallway appeared. It looked as if glass held the fire back. Frazier bounded through the corridor; Ernst shifted to vole and raced after him. They went through the fire and into the realm that held Aesa. As they exited, the flames overtook the hallway.

"Now what?" I asked.

"The case that holds her appears to be made of the same glass as the temporary corridor that Ernst just created to allow their entrance. It is big enough that if they crack it at the opposite end, Aesa will not be injured. I fear, though, that shattering the capsule will alert Geirrod. Therefore it is good that you stayed off that island. We must be prepared to hold off Geirrod and/or his troops until they return with Aesa."

My purpose appeared with crystal ball clarity. How stupid I'd been worrying about what Aesa would think if I didn't save her! How selfish! My focus and skills were needed here and not with Aesa. In readiness, I cupped my pouch. I would transform into a giant again and hold off the troops.

On the island, Frazier and Ernst shifted into boy and elf. Ernst raised his hands above his head and created a swirling ball. Then, he lowered his hands like a priest saying "Go in peace." Across his chest and between his hands, the swirling ball stretched into fifteen or twenty parallel lines of light. In one moment, one second's time, the lines of light became a glowing axe. Ernst took that glowing axe and smashed the lower portion of the case (the empty part); then Frazier crawled carefully through the shards of glass. When he reached Aesa's feet, he slammed his fist through the glass near her knees. As if by magic, the glass of the case split into two pieces and folded back like cardboard flaps on a box. Frazier lifted Aesa from the case with care. He leaped to the ground. He held her head cradled in his right arm; he bent his head down and spoke to her; and with his left hand, he swept her hair away from her eyes.

With that, Ernst pulled a wand from his belt. He waved it over Aesa's feet, then her mid-section, and then finally her head. As he shoved the wand back into his belt, Aesa's head moved. I watched as Frazier continued to talk to her and to stroke her hair. Then Frazier lifted her into his arms and walked slowly forward. Frazier looked at us, but he did not smile.

In that instant, Ernst shifted into the black stallion. Frazier helped Aesa onto the stallion and then hoisted himself up. Aesa's eyes appeared to be open for a moment, but then she slumped back against Frazier's chest. The black stallion found the highest flame; and I watched, in amazement, as the stallion reared just a bit and then calmly walked through the flame. They resisted the flames as if a force field had been painted onto their bodies. As the stallion entered the water, Frazier gripped Aesa with his right arm and gripped the stallion's mane with his left hand. Aesa, too, limply grabbed hold of the mane.

Egil spoke, "If the noise from the breaking of the casket alerted Geirrod, then this could be bad for Ernst, Frazier, and Aesa."

"Could the piranhas reappear?"

"Perhaps, but I believe that your fishing expedition has rendered the piranhas extinct, if you will. Let us keep a vigilant eye on them. Perhaps you should shift right now to be safe."

I watched Aesa, Frazier, and Ernst swimming to safety. I focused on them and how much I cared for them already in such a short amount of time. I shifted quickly this time as if my body could sense the urgency.

As they stepped out of the water, a voice boomed from the woods, "Who dares to retrieve that which is mine?" Geirrod and twelve giants emerged from the woods. I turned to face them, anxious to see how large I really was. Geirrod, the tallest of the group of giants, came to my elbow. As they fully assessed my size, they stopped in their tracks as if they had walked into a cement wall.

"Who are you?" asked Geirrod in confusion. I could see that he had not expected a giant of my size. He hadn't figured me into his equation.

"Who I am does not matter. Who you are is what matters," I spoke in riddle to buy us time. To my surprise, my voice sounded like thunder mixed with rain. It reverberated in such a way that Geirrod's cronies took two steps back. I thought, if my voice does that, then what might my feet do?

I decided to give it a try. I stomped my right foot and then my left foot. The ground in front of me, but not behind me, shook as if an earthquake had hit. Then, I dug my right foot into the ground like a bull ready to charge; this action prolonged the earthquake, but I think the sight of me caused more of a reaction. Two of the twelve giants stepped back into the forest and disappeared.

"Who are you?" repeated Geirrod. His voice sounded poised. I might have towered over them, but he knew that I was outnumbered.

This time I raised my hands and put them onto my waist as I spoke, "I am from the rock. I am nothing compared to he who made the rock. Beware of HIS strength."

The eleven remaining giants did not move: they did not retreat, and they did not charge toward me. Geirrod spoke in a whisper to them. I suppose he voiced his strategy. Slowly, they started to spread out, all except Geirrod. I suppose he thought he'd snatch those coming off the island while I was kept busy by his ten soldiers. As they approached, one thought kept repeating in my brain, "I've never fought anyone in my life." It was true. I'd wrestled but never been in an actual fight. Other kids at school had gotten in fights over silly reasons, but I was friendly with everyone and usually didn't even take sides in these fist fights. Usually, I'd tell those kids to quit being stupid and walk away. Having never fought a fight in my life, I wondered how I would do this.

Instinctually, I reached for my pouch. It made me think of my father, and he'd definitely been a fighter. I cupped my dad's pouch of wheat just so I could have a little strength from home. I could hear my dad saying, "Never swing first. If you counter, you always have the upper hand."

The giants surrounded me. The largest attacked first. He swung at me, but I hunched down. I took him and the giant behind him out with a double-leg take-down. Quickly, I jumped up and faced the rear attack...but not quickly enough. Two giants grabbed each of my arms, two giants held each of my legs, and Geirrod started racing toward me. As he approached his speed increased and he lowered his head. He became a speeding bull without horns. He rammed my stomach. I couldn't double over because of the eight-giant hold. I allowed the pain to reverberate up and down my body.

Out of the corner of my eye, I saw Egil bring a wand from his belt. I shook my head at him to let him know that I had this under control. He nodded back, but still he raised his wand. He flicked that wand, just as Geirrod raced by him; in the next instant, he tripped over a rock the size of my rock in my pasture. Instead of ramming my stomach with his head, he rammed into my shins with his head.

In a state of surprise, his cronies stopped, their holds on me loosening up. I needed but a moment to get the upper hand. I shrugged off the two giants holding my right arms like a kid shrugs off his coat. Then I swatted them like flies. They lay in the dirt next to Geirrod. Then I punched the taller giant holding my left arm. He slumped down but rose again. I gave him another punch to his left cheek, and he reeled backwards. Without warning the other giant holding my left arm let go. He didn't check on his friend; instead he stepped over him and took off for the forest.

Geirrod, still in the dirt, shook his head to try to gain equilibrium, so I took the opportunity to rid myself of the four holding my legs. I jumped into the air like a child about to throw the biggest temper tantrum of all time, and I did throw a tantrum...on top of the four who squatted down by my legs.

Once again I spoke, "I am from the rock. I am nothing compared to He who made the rock. Beware of HIS strength."

This time, the giants listened. They abandoned Geirrod in the dust. Geirrod's men high-tailed it back into the woods like scared puppies before a mighty lion.

"Cowards!" Geirrod yelled after them.

"Cowards? Yes," said Egil, "Dead? No. Perhaps, your cronies possess a higher intelligence than we first thought, Geirrod."

"Enough!" screamed Geirrod, and he disappeared into thin air.

I heard Ernst's voice from below, "You are even bigger than before! Amazing concentration and strength! In my 265 years, I have never witnessed such powerful presence of mind!"

I looked down at my friends and grinned, but I did not speak; for what I saw below caused my grin to fade quickly. Ernst was the only one looking up. Egil and Frazier were leaning toward Aesa, who slumped against a tree trunk. His eyes wide with worry, Egil looked at Ernst and then up at me.

Chapter 19

Calmly, Egil spoke, "Do not shift, young one. Ernst, she worsens. We need to get her to your tree."

Ernst refocused, raised his hand, and waved it over Aesa's body three times. He stopped for several moments and then stroked her cheek.

"True," he stated, "Kvist, we need you in giant-form. Aesa needs you to get her to my tree, or, I fear, we will lose her. My tree, old and wise in the ways of healing, is one of few trees who can deal with the extent of this poison."

Quickly, I lowered to one knee. I laid my open hand next to them. As they carried Aesa onto my palm, I felt a lump between my head and my heart. My heart beat so quickly that it felt like it spoke to me. She doesn't deserve this! Not fair!

As my heart spoke, I heard my voice correcting my heart. It is true; life isn't fair. I felt the emotion of the circumstances rise up to meet my reality. What happened to me happened beyond all odds. What were the odds that a rock spoke, that a rock transported a farm kid to another realm, that a pouch of wheat could cause that farm kid to shape-shift into a giant...what were the odds? For a moment, my faith shook, not like an earthquake, but more like when I'd move the dining room table several feet so that my mom could sweep beneath it.

"Listen," I said to anyone who might hear. "Don't hold my anger and my doubt against me. I may look like a giant, but I am just a boy."

I heard my father's voice reminding me that doubt and fear do not belong to children. "When you become an adult, then doubt and fear will creep into you. Until then, don't doubt or fear."

I considered my thoughts again and told myself, I am just a boy, but sometimes a boy can be a hero. My dark heart, in an instant, became light. Aesa weakens, but I can get her to Ernst's tree in time. I know I can. I have faith in myself and in Ernst and in the tree, so warm, so welcoming, so kind. I know she can mend Aesa.

"Ernst," my voice boomed, causing Aesa to stir, so I calmed it like my father calms his voice to tend to a baby calf.

"Ernst," this time my voice sounded like far-off thunder, "point me in the direction of your tree, and let's see the full-extent of my power."

Carefully, I placed them in the pocket of my work shirt. I kept my left arm in front of my pocket and used my right arm to shield me as I raced through the forest toward Ernst's tree. I raced forty-five paces; I knew this because I counted my paces to keep my mind off Aesa and her pain. Then I paused. In the pause, I heard a voice from my pocket, "I do believe that you sprinted to my tree in a matter of a minute."

I looked down and found Ernst smiling like a kid on Christmas morning, "Ernst," I said, "Astounding!"

"Exhilarating, if you will," came the next voice, and I knew from the "if you will" that it was Egil.

"Egil, are you all OK?" I asked.

"That is one question that I would love to answer. We are shaken but secure."

"How is Aesa?" I asked.

Ernst spoke with authority, "Set me in the crook of my tree. I will go locate my gurney. While I do that, you must gently lower Frazier and Aesa to my door."

I did as commanded. Being gentle was difficult: my index finger was bigger than Aesa. What an image! She lay in Frazier's arms in my hand. She grimaced.

"Aesa?" I whispered.

She opened her eyes.

"Listen," I said, and then I started to hum softly to her. She closed her eyes and the grimace softened. I didn't stop to think about my song choice. I just needed to soothe her, and even though I was a giant, I thought it might help. Eventually, I realized that I hummed the lullaby that I'd said to myself at the wall: "Down in the Valley." As I sang, my voice choked up like a stalling engine, for I remembered again my mother singing that lullaby. As I hummed and sang, I lowered my friends very slowly to the doorstep like a mother lowers a sleeping child into his crib.

At the doorstep, Aesa raised her head and said, "Thank you, Kvist. My favorite song. My mother still sings it to me sometimes." Even her tiny, pained whisper was a grimace of pain.

"Mine still sings it to me too," I replied in a whisper.

She laid her head back into Frazier's arms, and it was hard not to think of her as an infant. She exhausted much strength in her comment, for her head fairly dropped onto his shoulder. Her exhausted body went limp against Frazier's body.

Frazier took on his role of champion, "Aesa, please be still."

She whispered, "Be still and know."

I held my breath because if I had breathed, I think I might have cried, and a giant's tears were not appropriate at this time.

Ernst returned with the gurney; they loaded Aesa and wheeled her inside, and they shut the door.

Egil peeked out of my pocket and sighed.

"What can we do to help her? I feel helpless," I said nervously, and I couldn't resist the question, even though Egil knew it before I asked, "Has Ernst had a vision?"

For once, Egil did not scold me for my question. He spoke, "He can see only that we arrive here safely."

"Can we do anything?" I asked.

"We can keep ourselves busy. We can go to the kitchen and try our hand at the culinary arts."

"Why would we clean the kitchen at a time like this? Besides, Ernst's kitchen cleans itself!" I stated.

"Oh my goodness!" stated Egil with exaggerated emotion, "Culinary arts refers to cooking skills, if you will."

"Oh," I said and didn't speak again until I'd set him in the crook and shape-shifted back to the uneducated 10-year-old boy I sounded like. When I shifted, I landed at the base of the tree, and I hoped that Egil wouldn't come for me right away. My feelings were all mixed up like a strawberry banana malt: ice cream, malt flavoring, strawberries, and bananas; all smushed and mixed together, forced together in a blender by a punch of the puree button. I loved watching my mom blend them up, but today I felt like my brain and my heart were the strawberries and the bananas.

I paced around the tree. I gritted my teeth, and my hands became sopping wet towels that needed to be wrung out. Soon my teeth ached and my hands needed cracking. I kept pacing around the tree. To save my hands from more wringing, I reached out with my right hand and touched Ernst's tree. Still warm, I thought, and this made me smile remembering the warmth of her walls within the house. On my third route around the tree, I counted my steps and wondered how far round this tree measured. How big was it around the base? Was it an oak tree? If it was an oak tree, then did they call it an oak tree here in these parts? How tall was it? Was it officially the tallest tree ever? I walked around the base of the tree, examining all the details, lost in my wonderings.

On my fourth trip around, I ran my hand across the quilt-like pieces of bark and looked up. The branches of the tree shot out from the trunk and looked like the spokes of my bicycle tire. The canopy of leaves filtered the light, and for a moment, I stopped and smiled at the sure beauty of this tree. I lowered my eyes, and I continued my route with a silent speech, "Please let Aesa recover..." At the word recover my hand passed into an opening. I looked over to find a nook, an odd-shaped nook, for it looked like an egg that had been smashed flat on the bottom. The nook reached back into the tree about six inches. The flat end was a perch, and I sat down on it. My back, head, and arms fit within the nook, and my feet dangled over the side. I leaned my head against one side of the nook and closed my eyes. The rustling of the leaves sounded like a wind chime made of paper.

I opened my eyes and spoke, "Are you talking to me? If you are, then thank you for helping Aesa. Please let her recover." I stated this and felt silly because the tree did not speak like the rock. I giggled thinking that it must just be rocks that talked.

I leaned my head out of the nook and looked again at the tree's canopy of leaves. The leaves made me think of another lullaby that my mother sometimes sang to me. I started to hum "Rock-a-by baby in the tree top." It felt as if the tree rocked me; I knew that I sat still, but I opened my eyes to make sure that I hadn't moved. Again I focused on the rustling leaves; again I closed my eyes. Peacefulness covered me like those rolling waves lapping onto Loxney's shore. I felt like it was bedtime, my mom was tickling my back, and we were whispering my prayers. I thought I fell asleep and dreamed, but the tree spoke softly.

In the depth of my restfulness, I heard her. She spoke with youthfulness and yet wisdom of the ages; she spoke like a child, and she spoke like a mother to her children, "Listen, Young One, listen! Can you hear life around you? I am life! I have watched you, and you make me proud. You are a tree, too. You have been planted by the water and -- though you might doubt, though you might get angry, though you might feel jealousy, though you might be anxious -- you shall bear fruit in your season, and you will prosper. I am the tree of life. As such, I am like a human. I can feel, hurt, and make mistakes. You, too, are a tree of life. As such, you may have those feelings of inequity, but those feelings shall pass because you shall learn to not fret about them. This knowledge, this learning, shall come from your deep faith."

I knew I wasn't sleeping because when I spoke, she answered.

"Tree?" I asked.

"Yes, young one."

"I feel calm again."

"I know."

"Tree?" I asked again.

"Yes, young one?"

"Do you have a name?"

"Young one, you are the first creature to ever ask that question. Yes, I am Exdrasil. Thank you for asking that question," her tone was joyful.

My grin went past my ears again! I beamed like a car's headlight! I asked a good question!

Hearing my thoughts, she said softly, "All questions are good questions. Questioning leads to learning and learning leads to knowledge and knowledge leads to deep wisdom."

I paused here because my next question was a scary question but having been told that questions were good, I asked it anyway, "Exdrasil?"

"Yes?'

"Can you heal Aesa?"

"It shall take some time. I am not he who keeps this knowledge. It shall take some time. He, the great gardener of the tree of life, knows her fate, not I. Fill your mind, Young One, with all your blessings and give thanks."

The silence stretched out, replaced again with the rustling of the leaves. I did as she suggested. I focused on my blessings, and a movie of images passed through my brain: my parents, my brothers and sister, my grandparents, our ranch, our crops, our cattle, our house. The images continued: Geirrolf, Egil, Ernst, Frazier, and Aesa. I focused as hard as I could. I felt like my thoughts mingled with the rustling of the leaves and the filtered sunlight and the quilt-like pattern of the bark. My focus was tight like a sore throat. On and on I kept up my thought process from that nook.

"Aesa," I spoke out loud.

I clenched my jaw and my hands so hard that I think I fell asleep, but I don't think I was fully sleep. I know that doesn't make sense...

Egil's hand on my shoulder interrupted my prayer-like sleep. As I turned toward him, I knew that my eyes filled with tears. Hastily, I rubbed away my tears. I had never felt anything like this before. I felt healed, renewed, able to continue, and I knew without asking, that Aesa would recover.

Egil knew my question, knew my heart, and answered both, "Yes, she will be fine. She recovers in Frazier's arms."

His comment made my heart fall like a teeter totter, and it hit the ground hard. I had to shake my head side-to-side and up-and-down. So be it, I thought. I am not of this world. And I remembered what the tree had spoken to me. These feelings of love for Aesa will pass, or that is what my brain told my heart. Now, I waited patiently for my heart to hear my brain.

In a whisper, I heard the Rock speak, and it felt like he spoke straight into my heart, "Your heart is in your own world. Trust me, she will be worth the wait."

In that moment, I laughed and looked at Egil because I knew that he knew.

He smiled back and said, "Perhaps I will meet her someday."

I replied, "From your lips to God's ears," and then we both broke into laughter, the largest laughter ever. This laughter could have filled a small valley. With our arms about each other's shoulders, we entered the elevator which took us to Ernst's A-frame in the crook of the tree. Upon entrance, we heard laughter from the loft. Up the stairs I raced; my relief and my eagerness to see my friends propelled my legs up four steps at a time. I faced Frazier and Aesa with a fresh smile and attitude as if I'd just awakened to the sun shining into my window. She stood but leaned against his side, and his right arm held her waist.

"I am really glad that you are safe," I said, "I am really glad that both of you are safe."

"I am really glad that you came back to us, Kvist. We need you, regardless of Geirrolf's warning," Aesa said, and she read my face well. "You remember how he sent you away, how he told you to go back to Hansenville and never to return?"

I nodded, and she continued, "Have no fear, faithful warrior. Geirrolf wanted to send you home because he loved you instantly. He wanted you safe and felt that he could handle the treason in our kingdoms. As you can see, we needed you," and with that comment, Aesa stopped to catch her breath. When she looked up again, she said, "Geirrod's strength and abilities with the Art of Mischief have grown. This sleeping potion that he used on me was very powerful; I fear that I will be recovering for weeks."

Frazier scolded her, "Please save your strength. Please try not to talk, your highness."

"Yes, my guardian," she said and looked up at Frazier with an adoration that I have never seen before. The twinge that I felt was not jealously. I think what happened was that, in that instant, I came to fully understand that in Aesa Linnley Cecille Thorstensen was the continuation of this royal and rare line: the Thorstensen line was a rare gem. I think, once again, that I realized the importance of my purpose here in Roxsthroe. The Thorstensons were filled with goodness and mercy, and their intent was peaceful: I knew that I must protect this way of life for them and, more importantly, for their people.

"It is time," said Egil, "we must return to the twelfth kingdom to finalize our attack, especially since Geirrod knows now that we have a special weapon, a hidden warrior, if you will." With that, he winked at me and turned to Ernst.

Once again, they had a silent conversation. They looked like actors in a silent movie, only their mouths did not move. It was the best nonverbal communication I had ever witnessed, and I'd watched silent discussions between my parents for years.

Finally, Ernst said, "Fine. You are right. I'll get the berries. How often do I get to see a chosen one in combat." Then he spoke again with averted eyes, "Besides, I like this one," he said and referenced me with his arm and bony fingers.

We stood in a circle to eat our berries. It felt like church camp, minus the singing.

Chapter 20

I landed with my eyes closed, and I heard the sea. I listened to it with my eyes closed, and I couldn't suppress the feeling; I felt at home. I struggled with this for a moment. My home, a ranch, a land-locked place, in a different world, possessed waves of wheat not waves of water, but the sound of the sea seemed like home. Could it be that my ancestors, at some point, sailed or fished? Could it be that my German and Norwegian ancestors did not farm the land but harvested from the sea? I did not know the answers, and I knew I could not afford to ponder now. I would save this memory, though, and ask my parents later.

With that, I opened my eyes to the beauty of the sea. From our perch in that same cliff-side castle, the waves appeared to be in slow motion, but their echo suggested that they actually crashed against the shore. All the same, they appeared to be rolling in calmly creating peaceful waves. The waves spread out today with the same care as my mom takes when she spreads frosting on a cake. Methodically, she frosts from the left side of the pan to the right all the way down the pan, and then she turns the pan and makes waves of frosting from the top of the pan to the bottom. Mesmerized, I walked to the edge of the loft, half wishing for a parachute so I could escape for the morning and play amongst those waves.

"What are you thinking?" Aesa walked up next to me.

"Not thinking. I lost myself in the sea, and I wanted to go swimming in the waves," I said all of this without looking at her or those eyes; but finally I could resist the urge no longer, and I looked her square on and continued, "I know that is not possible, for we have work to do."

"Kvist, when we finish, I promise an entire week of play." She looked at the waves, too, as if she gathered her thoughts. Then she breathed in, and I wondered if she felt weak, but as she continued I know that it had nothing to do with her strength. She held back tears. I know that I'd only just met her, but I had a feeling she hated crying as much as I did.

"Thank you, Kvist. I knew that you would return; in fact, I knew it because I had such a strong feeling about you. Some worlds would call that a crush. Yes, I believe that I had a crush on you."

I stopped her with a stare, "I think the feeling was mutual."

"Do you believe in love at first sight?" she asked.

"I guess so. I don't really know though."

"I didn't," she said very matter-of-factly as if she answered a question like do you like broccoli?

Then she looked down at her feet and continued, "Until I laid eyes on Frazier. It is one of those things you can't explain like the amount of stars in the sky. In fact, I still doubt this feeling, and I wonder if it is just some trick concocted with the Art of Mischief."

I interrupted, "It is not the Art of Mischief. When I watched you with Frazier, I too had a feeling that this was to be. Something really real exists between you two. Obviously, we're not meant to be together."

"Well I don't," she said sternly and then her face softened.

"I don't mean to sound cocky like we should be together. It's not that at all. It's just that the rock spoke to me, saying that my love awaited me back in my world. You and Frazier are real."

She looked back at the waves, giggled, and took my hand, "This that we have then is a friendship so deep that different worlds cannot deny it. We shall remain in this friendship for a lifetime, maybe longer if permitted."

"Our fathers traveled through the rock as youngsters. Do you know when the rock quit working for your dad?" I asked, realizing that our friendship would last only as long as the transport magic would last.

"No. But Grandmother Linn says that it has to do with age."

"That's what my father said too, that it would end around age 15. Perhaps it doesn't have as much to do with age as with strength. Perhaps we can make it last longer?" I asked.

With our hands joined, she said, "Let's make a pact to try this. When all has been righted in our worlds, then let's live and laugh and love and work with such strength that we can make this magic work our whole life."

"Agreed," I said, and put my arm around her shoulders like an older brother does to a younger sister.

Egil broke our silent half-hug, "Young One, we have work to do. Save play for another day."

"Yes, sir," I said.

We turned together and returned to the group.

Linn spoke like a commander-in-chief, explaining the location of our troops versus the location of Geirrod's troops.

"Geirrod has taken Roxsthroe, Ringdom, Gerd, Dadivland, Bjornfield, and Valk. He has not retreated from the fifth kingdom, Valk, but since his encounter with Kip at the Island of Fire, he has moved his trips behind the border of the fourth kingdom, Dadivland."

She looked at me next and said, "Kip, you must understand the lay of our land. Roxsthroe, Ringdom, Gerd, and Dadivland, are all dominated by farms with about one-quarter of those lands covered by the Forest of Folke. Mostly, these plains roll, much like the land of your ranch. But, at the northern edge of Dadivland, rocks form buttes, pinnacles, and spires. These mix in with the grasslands and farmland there. I think these formations offer him and his troops protection from a surprise attack. We cannot attack them because we do not know for sure where they've hidden themselves. In addition, one-fourth of Valk is a mountain range called the Roseland Mountains. This mountain range, in turn, is yet another defense. That being said, it is a defense against us, but, if he is going to attempt complete control, then these landmarks become problematic, obstacles in his march to the sea. I think he wants us to attack him now, because he is within the confines, the safety of Dadivland's rocks and the Roseland Mountains of Valk. This is the most difficult place for us to attack and he knows this. His best chance at defeating us is there."

"I agree," said Ernst, "Alfaland, the sixth kingdom, Wigdahlen, the seventh kingdom, and Eddapo, the eighth kingdoms are our domains. We, the elf population, will fight him tooth and nail, and Geirrod is well-aware of that. Add to that the fact that our kingdoms are forests, forests that he has never taken the time to explore. The ninth kingdom, Verlen, would get him to the dwarfs, but Wallerland is ours as are Wonzington and Loxsney! If Verlen is his goal, then waiting for us to attack now seems the most logical. I agree, Linn, he wants us to attack him now. Don't you think that this fact, then, gives us time?"

"Indeed. We are in a good place…Forgive my word choice; war is never good. I am quite sure that he cannot attack us at Alfaland; he knows and fears the elf population. I think he sits and waits for us to attack him. He out-numbers us, but he does not know this. What we have on our side right now is time. With the magic of Laird and Geirrolf, we are no longer out-numbered; in fact, we might even have the upper-hand. His troops wait. He waits and while he waits, he questions Geirrolf and Laird about this new threat, about this blond-haired giant that he encountered at the Island of Fire."

Egil spoke next, "Of course, they will not speak. They probably sense that it is Kvist, but they will not speak to Geirrod or to each other. They know that Geirrod's magic is everywhere, and his greatest power is hearing."

I spoke up, "So it seems, then, that what we need most would be to retrieve Laird and Geirrolf, true?"

"Yes," Linn stated, "but Geirrod knows this, and with the appearance of the new giant, he will have made his fortifications that much stronger."

I spoke again, "Then, perhaps, we do need to be on the offensive. If we attack Geirrod's troops in the fourth and fifth kingdoms, then he will have to leave the castle of Roxsthroe to attend to his troops.

"I believe that the Young One is correct," stated Egil. "Geirrod would have to leave for battle. A small group of us could rescue Laird and Geirrolf while the battle ensues."

"I have to ask," I looked at Egil, "What does 'ensue' mean?"

Egil breathed in very deeply and said, "Young One, it means 'begins.'" Then he breathed out.

I looked at him, breathed in, and said, "Thank you kindly," and then I breathed out. Ernst's chuckle occurred at the same time as his knee slap.

Frazier raised his hand and asked, "Queen Linn, you said they out-number us. Can we withstand a battle? Can we risk starting a battle? What if we lose the battle?"

Ernst sided with me, "A well-planned battle, an offensive, can be waged without casualty for us for some time. If we can give that rescue group the right amount of time, then Laird and Geirrolf will be back with us to finish the battle and reclaim the throne."

"Frazier," said Aesa, "Ernst is correct. We can wage war without casualty. When we work together our strength in the Art of Mischief outweighs Geirrod's strength. We are more skilled than he. I believe that we can do this."

Elva looked at her daughter with great pride, "You've grown stronger than before."

Aesa spoke three words, "Love and friendship." Then she moved to her mother, took her hand, and said, "I love you, mother."

"And I love you," said Elva back to Aesa.

Queen Linn and Egil had a silent conversation with their eyes. Regardless of what they said and whether they agreed or disagreed, Linn had the final word, "We agree then, a planned offensive that will last long enough for the rescue of Laird and Geirrolf. Egil, take your team onto the outer balcony and plan your attack. Elva and I will strategize from here. Ernst, because you are a guest, you may choose which team you would like to assist."

"Linn, Egil's team came to me, and I assisted in the rescue of Aesa; I will stay with this team. Thank you, your highness."

When we left the room, I didn't feel like a 10 year old anymore. I felt anxious but patient, angry yet happy, prepared and scared. Maybe I felt like a grown-up soldier preparing for battle, and that thought made me think of my father who had been to Roxsthroe as a boy and had been to Korea as a young man.

Chapter 21

We waited to eat the berries that would transport us into Roxsthroe until Linn's troops hollered "Attack!" Linn's troops had quietly and secretly waded down the River Kormet. They waded the entire length of Valk. Once into Dadivland, Linn and Elva combined their powers and located Geirrod's troops hidden within a valley amongst the rock formations. This valley was not too far into the Rocklands, possibly only several rings of rock in. Geirrod's troops were surprised to say the least. Geirrod's troops, though, fought back valiantly and pushed the battle toward Valk and into an open field in this valley where the wheat had only recently been harvested.

This all happened while Ernst, Egil, Frazier, and I set our plan in motion. When the battle went our way, Ernst let us know, but when the battle did not go our way, there was silence. It was like watching a Husker game with my dad, with, frankly, too much silent time.

So instead, we tried to strategize. We knew that we would not have the upper hand against Geirrod at least at first, but we knew that we had the element of surprise: Frazier could shift into a human boy; Ernst could shift into the black stallion; and I was the giant that Geirrod had not planned into his battle equation.

We landed in the prison and crept toward the cell where Ernst had seen Laird and Geirrolf being held.

I spoke first, and, of course, it was a question, "Doesn't it feel like these halls are empty? Where are the guards?"

Egil responded, "For once, a good question."

I lowered my head, a little bit frustrated. Had he not said "for once," I might have beamed, but the "for once" stopped the beam like someone shutting off a flashlight.

"I have a feeling," said Ernst, "that Geirrod has emptied the castle of guards and sent them to the front. Geirrod stays, though, personally overseeing his enemies."

As he spoke these words, I shivered and said, "Let's just do this. Maybe we will work so quickly that Geirrod won't know what has hit him. Maybe he'll head to battle because he fears us so much. Maybe his troops will call him away, and this rescue will be the quickest in the history of...well...of Roxsthroe."

At the intersection, Egil stopped us. He stared me into silence; I began to prefer Ernst to Egil, but I tried not to think about it because I didn't want to hurt Egil's feelings. Once we quieted, Egil reviewed the plan. Reviewing works when one takes a test, but in rescue operations, sometimes review sessions are useless.

Such was the case with this rescue.

We entered the cell in the form in which Geirrod knew us best: Frazier, a golden retriever; Egil, an elf; and Ernst, an elf. I entered as Kip John Hansen, the normal farm kid, the son of Lester and Patty Hansen. We guessed that Geirrod had not figured out that Frazier could shift to a boy, that I could shift into the giant, or that Ernst could shift to a vole or to the black stallion.

We entered like church mice. At the entrance, we silently assessed. Eight-foot-wide decking outlined the square cell. Laird hung by his outstretched arms; his belt and hammer perched in a bird cage three feet in front of his face; and Geirrolf, in gopher form, perched in another bird cage behind Laird's head.

Laird's head rested on his chest: I felt a shudder, and sadness overtook my body in such a way that I had to turn from the scene for just a moment. Geirrolf the gopher slept: his head tucked between his front legs, and his tail tucked under his stomach. The sight of Geirrolf sleeping made my soul smile. I remembered! When gophers look like they are sleeping, actually, they are thinking deeply. I knew that Geirrolf readied himself for action. Instantly, I thought of our comradeship; I remembered how he told me to go home and never return; and I remembered Aesa's explanation, that Geirrolf had said what he said for my safety. I smiled up at my gopher friend. I wanted to help him, to make him proud.

Laird's bowed head nearly touched the top of the cell; and below us, darkness stretched for at least three stories. We knew that piranhas swam beneath us. If Laird fell, he would be devoured by them, yet the fall alone -- from the top to the water -- would probably kill anyone: gopher, dog, boy, or giant. As I peeked over the side, I heard the evil voice speak.

"Correct! I have filled the pool of water with deadly giant squid and piranhas. Where is your gigantic fisher? It does not matter because even he could not fish these out because there are hundreds, and you haven't the time, now do you?" Geirrod spoke these words with long pauses between "time" and "now." He had no clue that I was the giant fisher, the one who killed the 28 piranhas around the Island of Fire.

Slowly, I looked up to find Geirrod directly beneath Laird. Behind him, a plank of wood extended back and attached itself to the decking opposite of us. He had ridden the plank out over the pool, and he continued toward us. In addition, six giants entered across from us and headed toward us on the right-hand side. Why they didn't split is beyond me, but I saw an opening and I took it.

"Follow me!" I said, and we took off around to the right. My idea, my opening was a closing. At this point, Geirrod's plank changed directions and headed straight for us. In addition, the six giants appeared to become intelligent quite quickly because they split apart and three ran around the other side. Three giants surrounded us on each side, and Geirrod headed toward us.

Frazier shook, a frightened puppy, and instantly I remembered how afraid storms made him; and now, apparently, giants named Geirrod scared him as well. Geirrod saw this fear and aimed his mischief at Frazier first. Geirrod held his hand toward Frazier. With his eyes closed, Geirrod mumbled three quiet words. He put his hands together and then pulled them apart slowly, like someone pulling taffy. Then he opened his eyes and pointed at Frazier. We watched as Frazier floated off of his feet. He flailed his paws as he drifted through the air. Sadly, the flailing did nothing except prolong the inevitable. From the ceiling dropped another bird cage, and Geirrod locked Frazier away, hanging next to Laird. Three paws and fore-legs stuck out as did his tail, and his nose was squeezed up against the cage's door. Frazier let out a yelp as Geirrod started to rock the cage back-and -forth. Finally, Geirrod brought it to a halt.

"What do you think, Laird? Have you seen enough? Are you ready to remove yourself from the reign of Roxsthroe?"

Laird opened his eyes, long enough to look toward Frazier and say, "Dorg, I forgive you. Do not fear. We will prevail," and then he lowered his head again.

"No words for me?" asked Geirrod. "That will be just fine."

Geirrod positioned his hand toward me, clapped his hands together, pulled them apart, and sending his magic. I pulled the pouch of wheat from my shirt and cupped my hands under the it. His magic met my magic as I shifted into an even larger giant form. I watched as an explosion of white light occurred next to my giant tennis shoes. For emphasis, I stepped on the last spark. At the same time that I stomped, Egil saved the day with his hidden surprise. He shifted into the largest eagle that I have ever seen. He swooped toward the giants on our right. Off-balance, they fell into the water below. Their screams did not stop us. Egil rose above Geirrod's magic and perched on top of the cage which held the belt and the hammer. He cocked his head and stared intently at Laird's bent head.

Geirrod spoke, "One giant and one eagle? That is all? It would seem, Laird, that I still have the upper hand. Prepare to be dethroned!"

In this same moment, I stomped toward the three giants on our left. My stomping broke the part of the deck below them, and they plummeted toward the piranhas and squid. Ernst positioned himself in front of Geirrod. He pointed his wrinkly old hand at Geirrod and spoke, "Doom to you who incorrectly use our Art for Mischief! Be cursed!"

As the plank returned toward the opposite side of the room, Geirrod spoke, "Too late, Ernst. Your old-fashioned handling of the Art has made it obsolete. As I waste breath on you and this pitiful boy giant, my troops defeat yours. You may be able to rescue these fools, but I will reign supreme! Without you, we shall easily surpass Valk and be to your precious tree in Alfaland before the sun sets!" Then he disappeared.

His evil words resonated in our ears.

Frazier incessantly yelped from his cage. I knew he couldn't talk in that state. I knew he worried. I remembered that when we picked him up from the veterinarian clinic, the doctor had said that Frazier had been abused. No wonder he was scared of everything and had no confidence.

"Frazier!" I yelled, "Stop barking! Control your fear! We'll get you down. Have faith! Think of Aesa. Think of the lifetime of love that is in front of you."

At that comment, Laird lifted his head and spoke, "Aesa? Lifetime of love?"

Geirrolf, in gopher form, spoke next, "Apparently, Laird, we have missed quite a bit." Then Geirrolf focused his stare on me, "And since when can you shift to a giant, Young One? I do believe that you are larger than I."

Ernst scolded them, "Story time will have to wait, your highness. We haven't time. We must get ourselves to the battle at the rocks.

I smiled at Geirrolf and concentrated on his beard. I heard the rock speak to me, "Follow Geirrod...Form a bridge...form a bridge...follow Geirrod."

"How?' I said out loud.

"To whom do you speak?" asked Laird looking down at me.

"Laird? Can you hear me?"

"Yes, I have found some strength, thanks to the mention of my daughter's name and, of course, thanks to the 'lifetime of love' statement!"

"Egil, can you hear me?" I asked.

"Yes, Young One. You are in giant-form so we all can hear you quite well."

"Oh," I said, "I guess you are correct. Still getting used to this..."

Egil interrupted my rambling, "Kvist, focus. What shall you do?"

"I need to form a bridge. I can do that with my body. But can you figure out how to free Laird, Frazier, and Geirrolf?" I asked.

Egil turned to Ernst, "Can you shift to your vole form? I can fly you up here, then you can chew through Laird's ropes, if you will."

"With pleasure," said Ernst, "and without fear of my predator, the eagle."

Down swooped Egil. Ernst the vole stood up on his back legs. Egil landed and lowered his majestic head. Ernst chose the nose as his ladder and climbed on top of Egil's head in that way. Egil flapped his wings twice and was in flight.

"Crazy! Like the coyote and the calf together," I said quietly. What a sight to behold!

For a vole, Ernst must have had razor-sharp teeth because he sawed through first rope with ease and quickness. As he went to work on the ropes around the other hand, I leaned over the deck's edge and dropped like a board. My hands reached the other deck with room to spare. From the side, I looked like I performed a powerful push-up: my feet balanced on the one side; my legs and back formed a board across the pit; my hands balanced on the other side; and I held my head above the deck.

Laird fell and landed softly in the small of my back. Slowly, for his arms and feet must have been asleep and must have felt like 100 pound weights, he crawled along my legs and onto the safety of the deck. I could not see, but I knew that Egil and Ernst would not fail me. I felt two fall onto my back, one lighter than the other; and I assumed that one was Geirrolf, the gopher, and the other was Frazier the dog.

Egil spoke, "Young one, you may resume your position on the deck."

I pushed myself off the plank and into the standing position. Above me, Ernst the vole perched on Egil the eagle's head, and in Egil's beak hung the bird's cage which held Laird's belt and hammer.

Laird spoke, "What irony! The eagle flies with a bird's cage in his beak and his prey on his head! I believe I have lived a full life! What a sight!"

"I know. I just was just thinking about the coyote and the calf," I said and then asked, "What's irony?" In exasperation of another question, Egil nearly dropped the cage into the pit of giant squid and piranha.

He landed, transformed back to guardian elf, and smacked my giant calf in what seemed like one action. As he smacked my calf, he spoke, "Transform and ask no more questions!"

Ernst transformed and chuckled at me. I transformed as well.

"Irony is..." Ernst started to answer my question, but he did not finish. His face went pale like a pool drained of water. He looked off to the right and seemed transfixed.

"Ernst, what is wrong?" I asked, forgetting about the meaning of irony, "What do you see?"

"No time to tell," he replied, "Geirrod spoke the truth. The tide of the battle turns in his favor. We are losing. Quickly! We must transport to the sixth kingdom! Our troops have been pushed back into the forests of Alfaland. Be prepared to fight!"

Chapter 22

To transport takes only moments, but in those few moments, I felt like an insane bull locked in a head gate, nose bloodied from beating it against the metal bars. I stamped my feet, made fists out of his hands, and clenched my jaws. I closed my eyes and saw only blackness. I felt wrath. I didn't know what to call it until later, but I felt it all the same. In the second grade, I remember my teacher describing emotions using colors: sadness was blue; envy, green; and anger; black. I saw blackness, and then I saw Geirrod's face. My teeth gritted, and my hands clenched. I swear I shifted while I transported. I remembered what the tree had said that feelings would pass, but I figured this feeling of wrath would be with me until I defeated Geirrod or he defeated me. Yet through it all, I felt the purpose of the protector. Roxsthroe needed my protection, and I would provide it. When my eyes opened, we were steps from the front line; and Roxsthroe and its allies were behind us. In the matter of a moment, I took in the scene. I saw elves and dwarfs, giants and warriors, wolves and birds, deer and antelope, gophers and dogs, horses and buffalo, and monsters and dragons. There seemed to be no sides; all types fought on both sides. My eyes focused on finding Geirrod. I found him one mile behind enemy lines. Just like a lily-livered giant coward, I said to myself, to be far behind the actual fighting.

I said nothing, and none of my allies said anything to me. It took me 115 steps to run to Geirrod: with each step, I stomped out enemies; with each step, the earth quivered, knocking more of the enemy to their knees; with each step, I made a path through the enemy. Geirrod saw my advance, but he did not run. With his hands clenched into fists and set onto his waist, he watched me approach, and he felt my coming because each step caused yet another quake. He stood his ground, and my wrath propelled me forward. As I bounded toward Geirrod, I heard the Rock's voice, "This battle is a valley of darkness. You feel wrath for Geirrod but push that aside like you would push the waters of a great river as you maneuver down it. Remember your purpose. Do not fear. Do not doubt. Your are the chosen one. You are good and deep soil," and then he said, "Young one, use one seed of wheat...use one seed of wheat...use one seed of wheat..."

Once again I spoke back to the rock, "How?" but as I spoke, the answer came to me. I recalled my dad and I standing next to the grain truck, full of harvested wheat. My dad's hands were a cup full of wheat seeds.

He looked at me and said, "Take a handful. Put it into your mouth. Chew it and see what happens."

Curious, I tilted my head to the right side. I cupped my hands and put them into his. I threw the seeds of wheat into my mouth, and I chewed. As I chewed, I felt the wheat turn into something.

"It's gum!" I hollered, and my dad chuckled in reply.

I would take one kernel of wheat from the pouch to chew. I stopped in my tracks for two reasons: to retrieve the kernel of wheat and to fool the trickster himself. Let Geirrod wonder why I stopped. I opened the pouch, and found gigantic seeds of wheat. I took one seed between my immense index finger and my immense thumb. I put the kernel between my lip and my gum like farmers sometimes do with chewing tobacco. I held it there as I ran the rest of the distance. I wasn't sure what the kernel would do, but I figured I had better save its power until I stood in front of Geirrod, especially since Geirrod did not seem too frightened of my size.

As I ran, two giant figures ran beside me: Geirrolf, on my left, with his face grimaced and ready; Laird, on my right, with his hammer in hand. Together we approached Geirrod's lines of defense. His first level of defense was a line of smaller giants which we split into thirds. Laird disposed of his third with his hammer. Each hit of his hammer caused two giants to flatten, and their innards mixed with the dirt. Geirrolf used his fists: one slam for each of his assigned third. His opponents met with the dust and dirt as well. I took care of my third like an upset person emptying a table of its contents; I swept them off like cans into the trash.

Geirrod's next level of defense -- a circle of fire similar to the circle around Aesa's island -- was an easy fix. I watched with glee as Laird slammed his hammer down on the twelve o'clock position, and the fire exhausted like a line of dominoes.

Geirrod's third defense was another line of giants, but these giants were the brutes. We three were huge; in fact, we still towered over them, but they outnumbered us. To us, meeting this line of giants was like meeting the entire defensive line from a professional football team would be to three humans. They looked like they wore pads, but they did not. Their shirts were stretched across tight muscles. We looked at each other and were just about to step toward our task when we heard Linn's voice yelling, "Look out below!"

We looked up to see Linn, Elva, and Aesa, three golden triplets with three sets of green apple eyes and golden, harvested wheat hair. They rode in a chariot, pulled by Egil the eagle. We watched as Elva and Linn stepped to the sides of the chariot. Each wore a cloak of feathers. In fear, we watched as each jumped from her side of the chariot: there was nothing to fear though because these capes were wings which allowed them to fly. From their sides, they revealed colossal swords, swords as big as two-by-fours. With each swoop, they beheaded a giant.

Laird stated, "Isn't my wife amazing!"

We nodded. Then he said, "Let's get to work!"

We three fought hand-to-hand: good giants versus those powered by Geirrod. As I reached deep inside myself, I pulled beards and hair; I grabbed heads and broke noses against my knee; I tripped unknowing giants and pinned them to the ground with tree limbs. I thought, my fierce battles against my sister have paid off.

In the end, we prevailed, but Geirrod still stood in the same conceited stance with his fists on his waist and his nose and chin raised. Occasionally, he threw his head back and laughed. The sight of him laughing made my wrath grow. It felt as if the wrath would bust out of my chest. At that moment, I felt the seed of wheat lodged between my cheek and my gum. Using my tongue, I pulled it out and placed it between my molars on the right side of my mouth. It took me five steps to meet him face-to-face, but on the third step he held out his hand like he had done to Frazier in the prison, and he spoke a spell. Before I knew it, I ran on air. My gigantic feet had left the ground, and a bubble encapsulated me just like it had Frazier. I looked around and discovered that encapsulation had occurred four times: Laird, Geirrolf, the chariot pulled by Egil and holding the ladies, and me. Frazier and Ernst were nowhere near.

I looked down and discovered that Geirrod had encapsulated all of us and juggled us like a circus clown.

"Now or never!" I shouted and chewed the kernel of wheat. Suddenly, I felt a surge of energy much like my mother describes after her first cup of coffee in the morning. With that surge of energy, I lost all control. I punched at the wall of the capsule, and I broke through; I stomped at the wall of the capsule, and I broke through. Before I knew it, I fell, free-falling. I righted myself, falling like a cat.

Geirrod did not know what hit him; I had him perfectly pinned: my forearms held his forearms against the ground and my knees held his lower legs against the ground. His hands and feet were free, but he could only wiggle them a little. As I held him there, the capsules fell from the sky but did not break. They looked like bouncy balls. Laird's thumped a tree and broke; then he went to assist Egil and the ladies. Geirrolf's did not break, but he made short order of it.

They rendezvoused around me.

"In my world, we call this torturous trick the typewriter!" I said as I repositioned myself so that my butt held Geirrod's knees and my knees held Geirrod's arms. With my arms and hands free, I began "typewriting" on Geirrod's chest. Geirrod tried to growl, but his growl turned to giggles.

"Stop it!" he yelled, a combination of a man possessed and a small child ready to holler, "Do it again!"

"Say uncle!"

I heard Aesa giggle, and I heard Egil voice, "Focus, young one."

"Now that's how you wrestle! Down for the count, if you will!" exclaimed Egil.

"I'll sit on his legs for you!" exclaimed Geirrolf.

"Now what?" asked Laird, but mostly I think he wanted to kill Geirrod. He steadied himself with his hammer but continued to raise it above Geirrod's head just to let him know that the possibility of death loomed.

We watched as the battle dispersed. With their leader defeated, many quit fighting. Those mesmerized and still under the spell of

Geirrod remained sorely out-numbered. We waited; each of us hoping that the other had an idea.

From the battle marched Frazier the boy riding Ernst the stallion. Frazier dismounted and went straight to Aesa. Ernst transformed into his elf-form and marched straight to Geirrod's head.

First he spoke to me, "Young One, an awesome display of wrath! I'd call that Puritan style."

I couldn't resist, "So, considering how I felt, I can guess that wrath is pure hatred?"

"Yes, the Puritans believed God to be vengeful and full of wrath for us. Personally, I feel He is giving and patient and kind, but, I think, when the occasion calls for it, he gives us fury as a means and a purpose. That being said, Young One, I thank you for holding down this being."

Ernst looked at Geirrod and spoke quietly, "Geirrod, you said that my old-fashioned handling of the art had made it obsolete. Geirrod, this is not the case at all; in fact, my power in the art has grown. My transcendental nature, that of a recluse, has allowed for reflection, meditation, and the ability to achieve the sixth sense or four-fold vision. I am more powerful than you could ever hope to be. You will be cured of your cruelty, but you will not forget that my power reigns as the greatest in this land."

Ernst raised his hands above his head and swirled something into a ball. Like a professional baseball pitcher, he threw that swirling ball at Geirrod's left wrist. Chains appeared around Geirrod's left wrist and seemed to disappear into the ground. He did the same thing again, chaining Geirrod's right wrist, and again, chaining Geirrod's left foot, and again, chaining Geirrod's right foot. With Geirrod chained, I stood, releasing him from the typewriter; but I did not feel completely safe, so I did not transform back to a boy. Ernst created one more swirling ball and threw it at Geirrod's mid-section, chaining that as well.

Geirrod's face spoke his fear, and Ernst spoke, "Yes, Geirrod, it is true. Having achieved four-fold vision, I can bind you with chains that grow roots. You will live on here for as long as need be."

When I had wrestled Geirrod to the ground, his troops immediately laid down their weapons and dispersed. The Battle of the Rocks ceased.

Finally feeling safe, I transformed back to a boy.

Geirrod could not help but speak. "But you...but you...but you are but a boy!" he screamed.

"A boy raised on the farm in faith and hope and love. Geirrod, don't you understand the strength of those elements. You may win a momentary battle without them, but the life-long battle will not be won unless you possess them," I said this and looked at Ernst. He just nodded quietly.

Around Geirrod, a circle had formed. Laird and Elva were hand-in-hand, as were Aesa and Frazier. Geirrolf had shifted to gopher-form and had perched himself on my shoulder. My guardians, Ernst and Egil, stood one on each side. I thought it rather interesting that a circle formed around Geirod. A circle, the symbol of unity, formed around Geirrod who failed to understand the power of friendship. We had been unified in our defeat of him, in our defeat of the evil side of something called the Art of Mischief. I had so many questions about this Art of Mischief, but I'd kept them squelched; for sure though, I'd been keeping a mental list of questions. Pretty sure my list of questions rivaled Rip Van Winkle's beard.

Ernst looked around our circle of unity and answered one of my questions, "This circle that we have formed haphazardly, or sort of by accident, is the most powerful symbol associated with our Art of Mischief."

He looked around the circle at each of us, and then his eyes landed on Elva and Laird. His eyes rested on this couple for several moments of pride and then he spoke, "Do you remember the magical golden circle that I created at your wedding ceremony? Do you remember how I spoke of the child that I foresaw, who would follow in your footsteps, learning and living the Art of Mischief?"

Elva and Laird smiled at each other and then turned and nodded at Ernst. Ernst followed the circle. His gaze landed on Aesa and he spoke again, "Aesa, come and show your mother and your father what you've learned."

Aesa left Frazier's side and approached Geirrod's body. She held her hands in front of her chest, about 12 inches apart. She too formed a ball of swirl, and the swirl proceeded to her eyes like a small rivulet; then the swirl left her eyes and shot toward Geirrod's eyes like a tracker beam (but not like the ones used in Star Trek). Geirrod's struggling subsided, and he seemed to sleep.

Aesa slowly lowered her eyes and faced her parents. Laird and Elva wore their pride like fur coats. No words were spoken. Then Aesa encapsulated Geirrod's body just as he had done to her. In the end, Geirrod slept, chained, rooted to the ground, and encapsulated!

Chapter 23

Upon our return to Roxsthroe, we feasted. What a banquet! The buffet table reached five times the length of our dinner table at home. The table had so much food on it that I kept looking at the legs to see if they could handle the weight. The food, well, the fanciness of the food overwhelmed me. I've seen pictures, but I'd never seen an actual roasted pig with an apple in its mouth. At the dessert table, I stopped in awe of what appeared to be a layered cake, twelve layers high to be exact. I know this because I counted them twice.

As I recounted, Aesa walked up behind me and said, "It's twelve layers. My favorite layers are the cheesecake layers."

"There's cheesecake in it? I love cheesecake!" I exclaimed.

She giggled in reply and served me a slice. One slice took up my entire plate!

At first I ate, for I had never felt such hunger. Then, for whatever reason, my stomach shut off, and anxiety began. Was I homesick, or was I subconsciously thinking about parallels between Roxsthroe and the ranch? At one point, I left the party for the balcony and looked at their stars, but their stars made me think of my own stars on the prairie. I heard a creak and turned to find Geirrolf on the balcony with me.

He lowered his hand, and I walked onto it. He raised me to his shoulder. I perched there and looked out toward the stars.

"I am sorry, Young One," he said.

"For what?"

"For sending you home like a scolded school boy."

"Geirrolf, I liked you instantly, and I decided early on in our meeting that I would return no matter what you said."

"I realize that now. I hope that you didn't lose faith in me because I wanted you safe."

I touched Geirrolf's rugged cheek with my hand; my tiny hand took up such a miniscule portion of his cheek, "I have great faith, Geirrolf, and my faith in you will never change."

"Your marking suggests your importance to our culture, but if your power fell into the wrong hands, it could be used against us. We have knowledge only those who have used the Art of Mischief for evil, but we also know that a far greater evil lies ever near, an evil that we do not yet understand. This evil consumed Queen Linn's husband, King Lain, and it weakened him, shortening his life," Geirrolf paused.

I seized that opening.

"Besides," I said to him, "I need to thank you, for you saved the life of someone who I love dearly. You held her in your gigantic hand, but you held her so gently. For that, I must thank you."

"You've visited with your father then?"

"Yes. He told me the story of Queen Linn's husband. I think that might be why I feel so anxious, why my hunger shut down so quickly. I cannot stop thinking that an evil exists out there that makes Geirrod look like a mouse, and I need to rid my world of it before I grow too old."

"Then I can assume, also, that you had the conversation about age."

"Yes. He said that he returned to Roxsthroe once more, but by age 15, he could not go through the rock anymore."

"It appears to be true."

"Appears?" I asked.

"Since Ernst has achieved the sixth sense, it seems that perhaps travel could be extended. That being said, Laird, Ernst, and I would like to try to go back with you. Ernst believes that it will work because, well, he has seen us revisiting your windmill."

We paused as this information sank in.

"We also know that if something detrimental happens in Roxsthroe, then something equally as detrimental will happen in your land. In your father's time, drought ravaged your land; and flood attacked ours."

"So, I wouldn't have to fight this evil alone?"

"Absolutely not. We shall assist you, young one."

I literally breathed the biggest sigh of relief. I am pretty sure that the party inside the castle heard my breath. In addition, I think the breath made my food settle, allowing enough space in my stomach for one more piece of that 12-layer cake!

Geirrolf laughed at my sigh of relief, but we didn't walk inside; instead, we gazed at the stars again.

Several seconds earlier, Geirolf had used the word detrimental. I didn't need to be told the definition of "detrimental;" I could figure that out, so I said, "Here in Roxsthroe, a hurricane and Geirrod were defeated? What could be more evil than Geirrod?"

"Young one, that is why Laird and I would like to transport with you. We feel that together we three can prevent destruction, or at least together we stand a better chance. Ernst and Egil will travel with us. Is this agreed?'

"Agreed," I said, not caring about that cake as much as I cared my family. "Can we go now? I just want to get home."

Chapter 24

My friends led me to their rock. I lay down upon the Rock of Roxsthroe, a duplicate of the rock in our pasture. I carefully clutched the pouch filled with wheat seeds. I knew its power, and I knew that I would need it when I returned home.

Previously, the transport had been so relaxing; indeed, even in my anxious state, I felt its calmness again. For the first time, I called to the Rock.

"Rock? Please hear me. I feel frightened. I want my purpose, please."

Silence ensued, and the silence caused me to fret more. Then the doubting increased. What if the Rock can't speak anymore? What if the rock died? I answered myself. Rocks can't die. Why are you silent? This scares me, Rock. Please talk.

"Rock? Can you answer me? Rock?"

Only silence followed. Silence and calmness. Both enveloped me: I snuggled into the crook of something soft. I thought I started to hear something, and I jumped from the softness.

"Rock?" I asked, but he didn't speak, so I sunk back into the softness. It felt like my favorite blanket, freshly washed and line-dried. I fell now, further and further. It felt like sinking my teeth into a warm caramel roll. I fell far enough that when the voice started again, I did not jump; instead I just listened. Motion fully left my body; my brain shut down causing my thoughts to cease, and -- pretty sure -- that stillness only came to me in sleep. I did not sleep though. It felt like those few seconds before sleep hits, except the seconds had been stretched out into minutes. No thoughts and no questions, only feelings floating around like bubbles in a soft summer wind.

"Be still and listen...Be still and listen...Be still and listen..." These four words started very quietly, in a monotone voice, but by the end, these words formed a beautiful song. "Be still and listen..." Is it possible that I could hear the angels in Heaven?

Chapter 25

When I exited the Rock, I exited with that song in my ears and in my eyes; in my sight stood my mom and dad. I sat up and stood in one fluid motion; then I jumped into my father's arms. I felt my mother's arms around me; my parents sandwiched me in a hug, and I never wanted to leave them again. Yet, in that moment, I knew that leaving them would happen again and again because of Rosthroe.

"That's inevitable," I heard Egil say from behind me.

I twisted in my father's arms and looked back to find Ernst and Egil on the rock. You know how people talk about a wave of relief. Well, for the first time in my life, I felt that wave of relief when I set my eyes on Egil and Ernst. I knew that Egil had replied to my thoughts, the idea that I would eventually leave my parents. I jumped down from my parents' arms, but I kept hold of their hands.

"Thanks, Egil. With your help, my vocabulary will grow as large as Ernst's tree. Mom and Dad, meet Ernst and Egil. Mom, Egil is my guardian elf."

Egil stepped forward and shook my mother's hand. He said, "Please know that wherever Kvist resides, I reside there as well...no matter here or there." As he said "there," he pointed to the rock.

I could tell that the sight of elves had shaken my mom, but having heard Egil's words, her body relaxed. Ernst came toward her and did the unexpected. He hugged her, and then she wept.

"These are tears of relief," she said, "So sorry that I cry. I am such a girl."

My father grabbed her with a robotic arm; sometimes his affection seemed mechanical, but no one doubted his love for her. I feel it in his stare, whether that stare be above a grinning mouth or grimaced mouth.

"How long have I been gone?" I asked.

My mom looked at her watch, "We are in the sixth minute since you disappeared through the rock.

"Ernst, have you had any visions about the Hansen land?" I asked.

Instead Laird's voice answered, "I have heard from the rock," he said as he jumped from the rock and headed straight for my dad.

"The years have been good to you, Lester Louis Hansen." He stopped, and they embraced like two grown men with several inches between their chests, but stretched arms thumped each other's backs. Quickly then they stepped back.

Laird spoke again, but this time he spoke to my mother, "You, then, are the mother of this fine boy and the wife of this fine man?"

My dad said, "Laird, meet my wife Patty."

Laird said to my father, "Her eyes are so blue, ocean blue." Then he looked down at my mom, held her hand up to his mouth for a kiss, and said, "Pleased to meet you."

I watched this scene unfold and noticed Geirrolf in the background; suddenly he seemed kind of anxious. I couldn't stand the suspense any longer.

"What did the Rock say?' I asked anxiously.

"Lester, good to see you, but Laird we have a purpose," said Geirrolf, "and I can feel tremendous stress and electricity surrounding us. Please explain what the rock said."

"Yes, yes, yes. I apologize. We'll have time to talk later. We must save your land."

"I figured that was coming," said my father, "What do we have in store?"

"In Roxsthroe, Kvist saved the coast of the twelfth kingdom from a hurricane. We know that our kingdoms seems to exist on parallel planes. That being said, a storm moves your way. The Rock called this storm a string of tornadoes," Laird said.

"A string? How many? Is the string parallel or perpendicular to the ranch?" asked my father.

Ernst couldn't help but comment, "No forgetting that you two share blood. Questions...always questions, but questions are how we learn, how we fill ourselves with wisdom. Lester, my vision shows three tornadoes heading toward a blue house. My next vision shows three more tornadoes heading over a hill toward a metal flower tower. We must get to the blue house first...and fast."

As he spoke these words, we noticed the unusual calmness of the day, but this calmness came with an ominous weight. Humidity was a thick pair of wool socks. Clouds formed to the west and began to swirl. In this pause, I think we were considering what Ernst had said. Then it clicked.

My dad said, "The blue house is our farm house! Geirrolf and Laird, get us there fast!"

Laird shifted and joined Geirrolf in size and stature. Each lowered a hand; my mom and dad went with Laird, and Ernst, Egil, and I went with Geirrolf.

As we ran, the storm brewed, and the clouds began to swirl like a twisted cone, only this twisted cone possessed cold air going down and warm air going up, a tornadic combination. The sky split into two sections: one-half looked clear with just a few miniature marshmallow clouds; and the other looked like a gnarled mess of boiled-over marsh mellows, like Rice Krispy bars gone very wrong.

We spotted the ranch site as we came up the hill from the back. In front of us sat the house, a machine shed, and then the unattached garage. Past the house, the yard spread down to a small shelter belt of medium trees. Our wheat field followed the trees. Past the garage and machine shed, a larger, more expensive machine shed stood, and the cattle lots rested behind. When we spotted the house, I said, "My mom and dad built this house. They built it as they could afford it, starting with the basement. I slept in the downstairs bathroom until the upstairs was finished. Geirrolf, I am getting upset. You need to put me down now."

As Geirrolf lowered me, I carefully watched the rotating wall cloud. I saw one funnel slither slowly down the sky. Tornadoes work in slow motion. The funnel slithered a little ways down, and then it slithered back up. When it slithered back up, we breathed a sigh, but then it slithered back down just as quickly. Slowly it reached out and took hold of the ground; it looked like a farmer who grabbed a clump of dirt, broke it apart, and then threw the dirt into the air to see which way the wind was blowing. The tornado stayed down, and it threw up all that it touched.

"That's our wheat field!" I said, and I watched as its greenness exploded. Its stalks had just filled out their heads; this field was money in the bank, according to my dad.

The first funnel grew, becoming an old man with plenty of girth. To its right and to its left, skinny-man funnels formed, and together the three marched through our wheat crop, vomiting wheat seeds everywhere and mowing down stalks.

I wanted to cry, but I squelched the tears by cupping the pouch of wheat. "Be still and listen..." For a moment, I saw the beauty of the funnels, but that moment passed as I grew into giant form.

By this time the tornadoes hit our shelter belt, the electrical lines and telephone poles, and crossed the road toward our yard and house. Splintered wood shot out like spears and broken electrical lines were like fireworks on the fourth of July.

"Be careful! Watch out for wood!" yelled Laird.

Our front yard, an acre in size (Believe me. I know. I mow it with a push mower), looked small, like a mere sidewalk separating our house from doom. I watched as the smaller funnel on the right ripped our newer machine shed from its cement slab. I watched the tractors, the grain truck, the combine, and my three-wheeler get pummeled and thrown about like toys during a child's temper tantrum. The sound of twisting metal felt like an ear ache on my ear, but the pain propelled me. After the machine shed, the machinery, and the equipment met their end, the other funnel skipped along through our pasture, throwing our cattle about like rag dolls.

I moved like a gigantic football player. Remembering that in the twelfth kingdom, I dispersed the hurricane with a bear hug, I decided to push this storm back like a linebacker. I pushed it and pushed it and pushed it all the way back through the wheat field that it and its cohorts had ruined. Laird and Geirrolf did the same with the smaller funnels. When we reached the edge of the ruined wheat field, I called to my friends, "Let's stomp these out!"

I jumped above this funnel, above the cloud bank, and, for a moment, I surveyed the fluff above. How could something so soft produce something so destructive? This question I asked myself, but I did not take the time to try to answer myself; instead, I stomped on that tornado like a jump-roper, first with my left foot and then with my right...over and over and over...left and then right...left and then right...left and then right.

When the funnel died down into the ground, I stepped back as did Geirrolf and Laird. Before us were three black holes, and these really did look like the black holes that we study in science class. The tornado had been forced to funnel itself down into the ground. We could see the swirls and ripples of dirt and broken wheat.

We had time only to be thankful first for the safety of the family and then that the house and most of the buildings had been saved. We didn't even talk; looks of amazement, of sadness, of wonder, of happiness passed between us.

I turned toward the house and found my mother looking up at me. My mother beamed with pride like a candle in the window at Christmas time. I lowered my hand, and my mother stepped onto my hand. I held her close enough to my pocket so that she could climb into safety.

Egil hollered, "Ernst says we haven't any time. Tornadoes are headed toward your tower of wind. He transformed into the stallion, and he and Lester headed toward the tower of wind."

Only then did I realize that Ernst and my father had left this scene and headed toward our windmill.

"Same scenario," said Laird to Geirrolf and me, "Push these monsters back and stamp the life out of them. Which way to the tower?"

I picked up Egil, but I quickly pointed to the east with my other hand.

We moved in our giant forms, but when we arrived, a troubling scene awaited us. Three more tornadoes had formed and headed toward the uncles' ranch, and an added threat appeared. Amongst the outbuildings, human-size monsters made of swirling dirt sprouted from the ground. Their features, arms, and legs worked like real human features and arms and legs, but swirling, funneling dirt made up these features. My dad and Ernst fought with two a piece already. My dad, a veteran of the Korean War, could fight; I knew this through tales, but I witnessed a real fighter right there in front of my eyes. He punched with both arms like a boxer and street fighter mixed together. When one dirt monster grabbed him from behind, he took one punch from the other dirt monster, but only one punch. He shrugged his shoulders, and the monster holding him dropped his arms long enough for Lester to punch the one in front of him through the chest, in particular, through the heart. From the side, you could see his arm in front of, though, and behind the dirt monster. He held that pose for several seconds. With his arm through the heart of the monster, the monster disintegrated like grain through a grinder.

The battle on the ground continued (even my mom threw some punches) as the battle above began. The same scene faced us here as had faced us at my parents' farm. The funnel in the middle was the largest, and again there were funnels on both sides. They made their path toward the house through the pasture. I grimaced when the funnels tore through the fence that my father had been fixing yesterday. The funnels headed toward the uncles' barn, and behind the barn was their house, another smaller barn, and a shelter belt. To lose the uncles' house would be one thing, but, to us, their barn was more precious than gold. It was built like many farm projects, little by little and when time permitted. The building of it began after the Dust Bowl, after my father returned from Roxsthroe.

We met the funnels in the pasture. Laird and Geirrolf began pushing their funnels back into the pasture, but my funnel seemed to side-step me. Suddenly his large body curved around me, and I missed my tackle. I turned around, only to find the funnel ripping the roof off the smaller barn. I watched, in shock, as the funnel grew an arm and a fist and slammed the fist down on that barn. Then it sprouted two feet, one out of each side of the funnel, and another arm. As if it had read my mind, it twisted slightly toward the uncles' barn and house.

"My uncles live there!" I shouted to the funnel, and that thought propelled me to move. The monster turned and looked toward me, and I knew that I needed to get between my family and him; I would fight the dirt monsters. I faced him, juked to the left, but headed to the right. I deceived him (apparently he was not the brightest crayon in the box), and he sprawled to the left. This gave me enough time to get between my family and him.

I faced the funnel, its sprouted hands formed fists. I knew that, no matter what, I could not move because I had to protect my family, that house, and that barn...my heritage. I let that monster come at me.

I blocked his punches like a black belt in Tae Kwon Do: I used my feet, hands, knees, and my elbows, but nothing seemed to wear him down. I just needed one shot to the heart, like I'd seen my father do, but the monster punched relentlessly. One punch grazed the right side of my face, and I thought I might fall backwards, but I steadied myself. I tried to throw a punch, but the monster grabbed my fist and proceeded to squeeze it like a tennis ball. The pain brought me to my knees; I could not see out of my right eye, and he would not let go of my right fist. He took his left fist and punched my left ear. As he punched, the tornado spoke, "Beware Young One; we know where you live!" The pain and the statement brought anger to me, and for a moment anger replaced pain. Through the ringing of anger in my head, I heard Laird yell to Geirrolf, "Kvist needs help!"

I knew they approached, but I knew that they'd be too late. The tornado monster grabbed for my pouch of wheat, so I reached up with my left hand and grabbed for his left fist. Now we were locked in a death grip. He squeezed my right hand, and I squeezed his left. I would not let go. If only I could cup the pouch, I thought. When I battled the hurricane, cupping the pouch made me stronger. If only I could eat a kernel of wheat – that had made me strong enough to defeat Geirrod. Then I thought, I can't cup it, but I could pretend cupping it. I gripped onto his left fist with all my might; I closed my eyes and imagined my hands cupping the pouch of wheat; and I concentrated. I pictured a sheath of wheat blowing in the wind, all brown and golden and ready for harvest. I pictured my father's hands cupping the wheat. I felt the seeds of wheat in my mouth, and I chewed them into gum.

I didn't grow in strength literally; instead I grew in numbers. My grip on the tornado's left hand had held him off long enough. Geirrolf grabbed the monster's left fist and squeezed his entire arm with all his might. Laird approached the right side with his hammer raised; he smashed the tornado's right fist, and the tornado released my fist. Finally, my right fist was free. Then Laird grabbed hold of the creature's right fist and squeezed in a similar manner. Both of them grinned at me, as if together we had pulled the best prank ever. I wasted no time; I had learned from my father. I took my bruised right fist and I slammed it into the tornado's heart. First the arms and hands dissipated and floated into the body of the tornado; then the body melted down like the wicked witch in the "Wizard of Oz;" finally the feet collapsed. All that was left was a big twisted pile of dirt.

Near the twisted pile of dirt, I saw Grandpa Jack. He was being held down by a dirt monster. I reached down with my giant hand and flicked that monster into dust like someone flicks away a mosquito. Using my index finger and my thumb, I helped Grandpa Jack get to his feet.

"Thanks, big fellow," he said, and I nodded. Then, I looked back at the dirt pile created by the gigantic funnel.

Next to the dirt pile stood my father, my mother, my grandma, my uncles, Egil, and Ernst, and they shared the exact same smile. They had learned from my dad too; they had followed suit; and they had defeated the human-size dirt monsters. Finally, I felt that I could shift back to being a boy. Laird shifted as well, but Geirrolf remained in giant form stating, "Just in case."

"What did that tornado monster say to you?" asked Laird.

"It doesn't seem to matter right now," I replied

"Oh but it does, Young One," said Egil. "As your guardian, I am responsible for you, and you will tell us what the tornado said."

"You know," I said to Egil. "Your ability to read minds is not always convenient."

"Tell."

"Fine! It said: 'Beware Young One: we know where you live!'"

My mom stepped up behind me and wrapped both of her arms around my neck. I felt her strength, and she said, "There is nothing to fear, Kip. We will not let anything happen to you."

"Indeed, we will not," stated Ernst. "I believe I have some sort of solution. Egil, you can be a guardian for two: Laird and Kip. I know this. You did it in the past, but this will be difficult doing it for two different realms."

"This is true, Ernst," said Egil, and I knew that Egil and Ernst had already had this conversation in silent form.

Ernst continued, "I have eyeballed this amazing tree, old and huge, at the end of the gravel. It is an oak, and it has agreed that I may make it my home. If we are in agreement, then I shall set up my new residence there on the Hansen ranch. Is this agreed?"

All agreed with nods, except Egil.

Egil spoke with great solemnity, "I shall agree under one condition."

"What is it?" I asked.

"Funny YOU should **ask**," he said putting a hand on my arm. "My condition is this: you may ask only ten questions of Ernst per day!"

I rolled my eyes, but everyone else laughed.

In an odd sort of unity, we made a circle again around that large black hole like we'd made around Geirrod at the conclusion of the Battle of the Rocks. Adrenaline had hold of my body, yet I felt numb too. I felt like I had won the state wrestling title, but all the events afterward moved in slow-motion. I watched Geirrolf the giant approach my Grandma Malinda. He knelt down on one knee, put his hand on the ground, and my Grandma stepped onto his hand. He raised her up to his face, and I watched them chatting and laughing as old friends. I smiled deeply, for I knew that Geirrolf had saved her life. Laird and my dad stood side-by-side, talking and occasionally kicking at the black hole; both had furrowed brows. Ernst and Egil talked with my mother. She looked so comfortable with them, perhaps because she understood well the tasks and endeavors of those who guard.

I sneaked away from the circle and headed toward the barn. I sought out solitude in our three sectioned barn. The inner section was highest, probably 10 feet higher than the two outer sections. It looked like a normal barn, wood and metal, I thought to myself as I pushed open the side door. Inside, the smell of alfalfa, sort of sweet, made me breath in deeply. I walked through the one section and into the middle section. I looked up into the rafters. It reminded me of a cathedral I'd seen once in a picture.

I didn't hear my dad walk in behind me, but two feet behind me I heard him say, "It took Uncle Ted and Uncle Skinny one year to build this barn. Grandpa Jack helped them when he could. Yep, a whole year, but that's how farm projects go. You fit in the building of the parts around the big seasons: calving, planting, and harvesting."

"It looks like a cathedral," I said.

He chuckled and said, "It feels like a cathedral. We still do some praying here now and again. Back in the early days, we calved out and kept the calves for one year. In that year, we'd wean them in the fall, feed them hay in the winter, feed them grass in the summer and then we'd sell them. We rolled the hay into this middle section and feed yearlings on both sides."

We paused. Hansen men live, breath, pause, and occasionally talk. Hansen men weren't much for words, so I felt like the pause was necessary, maybe even deserved.

"This is a monitor style barn. Made it easier to roll the hay into the middle."

We paused again. In that pause, I realized that my dad was trying to thank me. All the while he talked, he never moved forward to stand by me, so I moved back by him.

"Didn't you help them shingle?" I asked.

"Yep, and ended up stepping on a nail in a board and getting a pretty good infection," he said.

"Thanks, Dad," I said.

"No thanks necessary," he said, "Let's head back, little hero."

We rejoined the group to hear my mom inviting them all back for a picnic by the rock the following day. With that, the Roxsthroe group headed toward Grandpa's house, since Grandpa and Grandma's roof, the one which I had landed upon after my initial trip to Roxsthroe, allowed them to return to their kingdom.

Uncle Skinny said, "Better take my pickup," and then he and Uncle Ted went into their house.

We piled into the pickup and headed home.

Chapter 26

That night, when my parents tucked me in tightly, I decided to ask the question that had plagued me the most. Mom sat up close to me, moving only to pull my comforter back because I only like the sheet, and my dad stood by the window and stared toward where the machine shed had been.

I sat up and said, "Too bad magic can't fix the shed." Slowly I worked my way up to my actual question.

My dad nodded in agreement, but he didn't answer me with words.

"Dad?" I started my series of questions carefully, "Remember how you told me the story of your trip in Roxsthroe?"

"Yes."

"Well, remember how Linn cried when you left?"

"Yes."

"Well, Laird brought the rain with his hammer, but Linn's pure gold tear drops landed in that cream can."

He turned and looked at me to answer, "I never knew for sure, but I always thought Linn's tears made the gold. Yes, I believe those gold pieces were her tears."

I let the silence settle a bit, like dust on a gravel road after a car drives by. I counted to 60, and at 61 I sprang with my question, "What did you do with the golden teardrops?"

"Funny you should mention those golden teardrops. I, too, have thought about them. To answer your question, we used about half of them to set up after the Depression. The other half, we buried, just in case of an emergency."

"Dad? Isn't this probably an emergency?"

"Nope. You should know your dad well enough by now. Those Morton buildings, the machinery, the cattle, and our wheat crop...all covered under insurance."

Not being one for much emotion, he uncomfortably tussled my hair and left the room.

After prayers, my mom said, "Don't you dare be scared. Be patient. This day was crazy, and he needs to get his brain wrapped around it. We will be just fine. Our safety outranks the importance of anything and everything else."

I turned over on my back, snuggled into my blankets, and my mom tickled my back. As she tickled my back, I felt like I transported through the rock. Between being awake and asleep, I could have sworn that, sometimes, the rock tickled my back too. I fell asleep thinking of the rock and feeling my mom's soft tickling.

Chapter 27

The next day, we met by the rock for a picnic. We ran to town to borrow extra tables from the church. My mom set up her usual feast: roast beef, mashed potatoes, gravy, corn, Jello salads, and lettuce salad. My uncles, including Uncle Skinny, attended as well as my Grandpa Jack and Grandma Malinda. From Roxsthroe were Linn, Laird, Elva, and Aesa, Geirrolf and his parents, Egil and his wife (who knew that he had a wife), Frazier, and Ernst. Frazier and Aesa had transported together, holding hands, and the hand-holding continued throughout the picnic; at one point, they went on a little hand-holding walk.

Egil approached me and said, "Obviously you are a bit upset by this."

I replied, "It was a heck of a lot easier for Luke Skywalker."

"Excuse me?" said Egil.

"Oh, it's a movie with a similar plot. Luke thinks he likes Princess Leia, but Leia likes Han Solo, and, in the end, Leia and Luke are twins. It would be easier if Aesa and I were brother and sister, separated at birth," I paused, and then added, "Don't worry, Egil, I'll survive. I'm too young for love anyway."

Egil replied, "Symbolically speaking, you and Aesa share a connection rather similar to that of brother and sister."

In reply, I shrunched up my face and shrugged my shoulders like the Beaver in the *Leave It To Beaver* television series.

I looked from the love birds to Egil and realized that he was laughing uncontrollably in reference to my Star Wars' plot summary and my grimace. When he had somewhat regained his composure, Ernst said to Egil, "Well, at least it wasn't stated in the form of a question." This caused Egil to break down into laughter once again.

I chuckled as well, realizing that Egil probably always had held and always would hold the right answer. Aesa and I did share a similar relationship to twins separated at birth.

We moved back to the main table where the discussion held weight like a dumbbell.

My dad asked, "Where did those crazy dirt monsters come from?"

Laird looked at Geirrolf and said, "Not sure."

Linn spoke next, "Lester, Ernst has reached the highest level of the Art of Mischief. He thinks that this magic comes not from the Art, but he can't be sure yet."

My mom looked at Linn and spoke quietly, "My husband told me of his adventure in Roxsthroe. He told how a strange poison infected your husband. Did you ever decide what it was or where that came from?"

Linn spoke quietly and calmly back, "No. Last night we sat up late trying to determine if the two shared a link. We are not sure, yet, but we have archives of books to examine as a means of determining the cause. We will start our examination of those texts tomorrow and, via Ernst, we will keep you informed. I believe that you will be safe. Your son can shift into a giant, and Ernst can see the future."

My mom and Linn shared a smile of understanding.

Geirrolf spoke next, "We know that this much is true. Whatever this evil is, it knows and seems to understand the magic and the power of the pouches."

As he said this, I cupped mine and then stuffed it inside my t-shirt.

Geirrolf continued, "Laird keeps his, and Kvist possesses his, but there may come a point where we will need to hide both pouches for safe-keeping. When and where will have to be figured out as well."

Laird continued, "Our purpose becomes figuring out what caused this, locating it, and eradicating it."

"What's eradicate mean?" I whispered to my father.

"Get rid of it like a noxious weed."

"Am I safe, dad?"

"With me around? Ain't nothing getting near you."

"Can I travel back to Roxsthroe? Aesa, Frazier, and I agreed to visit the sea."

"Later, but not until we have figured out who or what caused the dirt monsters and that damn tornado," stated my father, and I knew no budging would be allowed. I would remain on the ranch until the evil had been eradicated

My mom hugged me then and repeated her advice from bedtime the night before. "Be patient," she said and in addition, "Be still..."

The sun set behind the rock, illuminating it as South Dakota sunsets tend to do. Against the horizon, the rock grew black; behind it shades of orange stretched into pinks and yellows and blues and grays. As the sun continued its descent, the party broke up. Aesa and Frazier had been lost in their own world. Then each approached me separately. Frazier came first.

He stepped next me and spoke in one fluid moment, "What you said to me, by the Island of Fire, I heard every word. You said I had been called to save you, and I did that; in fact, when I fell through, the rock told me that he searched for another. When he spoke of what he needed, I knew he meant you. I think the rock sensed my answer, and he called you. Yes, and then you said that I had been called to save Aesa; I believed you. You said, 'Frazier, this is your destiny.' I may not know much, but with Aesa's help I will fully understand more. Kip, she teaches me already."

He paused, but I didn't speak because I didn't quite know what to say. I felt like the time my mom started crying because her daddy, my grandpa Sal, was really sick.

The pause ended quickly (thank goodness), and Frazier continued speaking, "When we rescued Aesa, when Ernst cracked that capsule, when I held her in my arms and she opened her eyes, I knew that she had become my purpose. I knew, in those few instances, that I would not let anything happen to her. When I told her how I felt, she admitted that she felt the same."

He paused again, looking at the rock, but this time I knew I should just wait. I needed to be still and be patient, just like my mom had told me.

"Anyway," he said, "I can't come home right now. I have so much that I can learn from my friends in Roxsthroe, not that I couldn't learn from you as well, but I want to learn it from them."

I let the pause go for a minute, just for effect, you know, and then I said, "Then it is agreed! You shall stay there and protect Aesa, and I shall visit once the evil has been squelched!"

Frazier visibly relaxed. He remained the same being that we brought home from the pound, always just a little bit nervous and scared.

As he left, Aesa approached.

Jokingly, I said, "You know. You owe me a day at the sea. I will not forget that little date. Even though you have fallen head-over-heels in love, you will be going on a date with me."

Her last few steps were a run, and she grabbed me in a hug, whispering, "Thank you so much!"

"Why?" I said, "I think I should be thanking you. Without the help of Roxsthroe, our ranch and our family would be destroyed."

"I thank you for what I saw, witnessed, in you. Your courage, strength in faith, your ability to face your fears, knowing that the end result might not be what you wanted: all these qualities make you an extraordinary human. Even your questions have taught me so much. When I stepped toward you just now, I knew that you could reject me, but you didn't. It takes such strength to watch someone you like fall in love."

"Aesa, my friend, my place is not with you," I said repeating the Rock.

She hugged me again, "I have not forgotten our date at the beach. I look forward to playing at the sea. When this evil has been discovered and uprooted, then we shall have you visit often. And remember, we agreed to make our friendship last a lifetime. Agreed?'

"Agreed," I said, and I released her.

Chapter 28

I couldn't sleep that night. I tossed and turned for what seemed like eons, but then I looked at the clock and only twenty minutes had gone by. I lay flat on my back, arms bent and hands behind my head. I stared at the ceiling trying not to think about anything, and in particular, trying not to think about what that tornado had said.

"Too late," I said out loud, and then my heart pounded as fast as my brain. I felt what must have been fear in the pit of my stomach because I felt like I needed to run to the toilet to throw up. I lay as still as possible, but I soon realized that my hands shook. When I'd fought that tornado creature, I felt no fear; only wrath. Why now, safe in my bed, did I feel fear?

My mom popped her head in my room and said, "Who talks in here? You?" she said pointing at me accusingly. But then she giggled.

"I'm awake," I said in sort of a moan.

She walked up next to my bed and said, "Scoot over, please. Scoot. Scoot. Scoot."

I shifted toward the wall.

She smoothed my hair and tickled my arms, "I suppose that you can't stop thinking about all the happenings. It's probably hard not to think about all that has happened. That being said, I suppose that you keep coming back to that tornado: what he did to you and what he said to you."

As she said this, she ran her hand softly over my blackened eye. Then she lifted my swollen hand and kissed it. Instinctively, I sat up and hugged her, kind of hard. I felt her tighten up, and then I heard her crying. I meant to say that she shouldn't worry, but I couldn't because tears seeped slowly out like oil on the side of the oil can. We hugged and cried for what felt like twenty minutes, but really only two minutes had passed. My mom pulled away first. She held the back of my head with her left hand and cradled my chin in her right hand.

"I want to clarify something," she said rubbing the side of my jaw with her thumb. "I am not crying because I am scared of that tornado. I am not scared of it, nor am I scared of whatever evil created it."

She hugged me tightly again and said, "I am crying because I am so proud of you."

She spoke that sentence with a crack in her voice; the sentence was a sidewalk, and her voice saying it caused the sidewalk to crack just a bit.

"I know, mom," I said.

She pulled back again, "Do you really understand? I have no fear in this matter. I have only pride in my big little man! A mom's pride is almost as big as her love, kind of like the cream can compared to a grain bucket. It's almost as big!"

"Thanks for believing in me, mom," I said, and we hugged again. We rocked back and forth for a time like a rocking chair on a porch when a little wind comes along.

I think I fell asleep on her shoulder. Once I felt drool leaving my mouth. I sucked it up quickly. Then my head started to nod off the side of her small shoulder. I caught myself. Finally, I felt as relaxed as a fluffy bed sheet drying in the wind.

When she laid me down, I felt the pillow, but I don't think I could have awakened if I'd tried. My body had over-powered my mind. The questions stopped; the memories subsided; and the voice shut down in my brain. I curled into this sleep like a piece of hair curls in humidity.

Then, I was at the ocean again. The huge waves somersaulted like football players. I sat in the sand and listened to the pummeling that the beach took. Before my eyes, a man, a very huge man, came walking out of the ocean. He wore a long robe. He had dark skin but sparkling blue eyes. As he approached his long hair flew out to the right and then settled down his back again. He waved at me and smiled.

I smiled and waved back. I felt as though I knew this man. Though I'd never seen this man before, I felt as if we'd spoken many times. I stood up in the sand. When I realized how huge he was, I reached up and cupped my pouch. When I shifted this time, I actually felt it in slow motion, and I enjoyed every second of it, just like when I pinned a guy for the state championship. I met the man in my giant form, but, even as a giant, I remained boy-sized next to him!

He smiled down at me and ruffled my hair like my dad ruffles my hair, like I used to ruffle Frazier's fur. He bent down on one knee and said, "Young One, you are blessed. You are watchful and you wait, like a faithful servant, like when you watch the cattle's gate. Do you know this of yourself?

"Not exactly," I said. "I try to understand, but my mind fills with more questions, and I doubt myself sometimes."

"Young One," he said with a smile, "you may not yet know this of yourself but your heart knows it very well already. For these qualities, we count you good and strong. For these qualities and many others, you are good and deep soil."

"Who are you?" I asked. "I feel as though I should know you."

"You know me better than you know your parents, your siblings, or your friends. You know me well. We have spoken often. Today, though, I bring you a gift. Ready yourself to receive it."

"Yes," I said, and I did not ask questions, even though my questioning ability remained intact and unhampered by the dream-like state.

"Hold out your hand. Close your eyes and count to 100. Do not ask questions. Your gift, small enough to fit in the palm of your hand, carries much power. Use it! Use the pouch!"

I felt his hand brush mine, and then I felt something land in my hand, but I started to count to 100. I did as I was told. I did not move my gift. I held my hand flat, as flat as a Corelle dinner plate. I didn't open my eyes until I hit one hundred and two.

I opened my eyes and looked at my gift. There in my hand lay a rock, similar to my rock in the pasture. I smiled at the man's back.

I hollered, "Thank you!"

The man raised his hand in a wave but did not turn around. I sat there watching the waves and turning the rock over in my hand. The waves rolled on, and a voice could be heard in the ocean, "He is the Rock, his works are perfect, and all his ways are just."

When I woke the next morning, I said out loud, "He is a Rock, his works are perfect, and all his ways are just." Then I sat up and realized that I actually held a rock in my hand, the rock from the dream.

Chapter 29

The next month passed quietly and peacefully, like a four-day weekend during school with no big events. The possibility of evil persisted, but evil made no appearances. As a family, we found ourselves regrouping and repairing our world. I suppose I expected to see my parents in a constant state of worry, but happily -- probably to the point of being ecstatic -- they went about their ranching business.

I asked my mother about this extreme happiness, "Mother, you and father seem really happy, maybe too happy. I thought you would be worried more. I mean, I am happy, but I'm a kid. I thought adults worried more?"

She turned to me, lifted my chin with her index finger, and said, "Safety matters the most. Safety brings on happiness."

I crinkled my brow. I wasn't confused, more puzzled. For a second, I recalled how the field of wheat had exploded. For me, that recurring image caused worry. I wondered what was the matter with them? Safety wouldn't replant the wheat crop.

She tapped her index finger under my chin and continued, "Earthly possessions are just that, of the earth. Our souls matter most, and our souls survived safe and sound. Yes, your father and I fret, but we could have lost everything. Fretting occurs momentarily because it is of this earth. This," she stated swinging her arms around the ranch, "is just earth. Our souls last forever and should know nothing of being fretful. Life, a gift, extends beyond death!"

After that conversation, I decided to let their happiness overtake me. I didn't drown in it. I swam across it, letting it lift me. But with worry gone, curiosity filled me once again; I was a fountain of curiosity. I kept it corked as long as possible.

One day, my curiosity concerning the Art of Mischief could not be contained. I knew that I wanted to see Ernst. I walked into our kitchen and said to my parents, "I want to go visit Ernst. How should I do that?"

"What do you mean?" asked my dad. "Wouldn't you walk or take the three-wheeler?" He chuckled as he finished, and so I explained myself.

"I mean, do I go unannounced? Should I go first and ask permission? You know? How should I do it?" I asked.

My mother, a really smart lady, had a simple solution. She said, "I have wanted to visit him too. Let's make some chocolate chip cookies and take them to him as a treehouse-warming gift."

"Perfect!" I exclaimed and hugged her waist.

We arrived at the foot of the oak tree. I searched the base looking for a door.

"No door," I said.

My mom and I looked at each other; confusion tickled my cheeks.

She nodded at me, smiled, moved toward the tree, and said, "I guess we knock."

She knocked on the bark of the tree five times.

Instantly, the oak tree tripled its height and its width. In front of us, appeared a door-sized knot in the tree. On the knot appeared a hammer for a knocker! I lifted the hammer as high as I could and let it fall. It knocked on his door five times. We waited for three minutes. How do I know that this? I counted to 60 three times in my head.

Then, the door opened and Ernst appeared, stating, "I knew you'd be arriving."

"Of course you did," I said and then turned toward my mom and said, "Ernst can see the future."

"Actually I predict the future," he said and beckoned for my mom to enter. "Follow me, we'll need to take a little ride to get to my new living arrangement."

On the elevator, my mom became me, full of questions!

"How did the tree grew?"

"Magic," replied Ernst without looking at her.

"But I just drove by this very tree earlier this afternoon, and it was normal."

"I know," said Ernst.

"But how did it grow? Will it stay this size? When will it shrunk?"

Ernst chuckled and looked at me, "Here we thought your innate ability to question came solely from your father; indeed, I believe that your mother's genetics are to blame as well."

I giggled, grabbed Ernst's hand, and said, "I am glad to see you."

He looked at me, eye-to-eye, as his full-elf size was the same as my ten-year-old size, and said, "Glad to be seen."

Then he turned to my mother and said, "When I decided to stay with you here in Hansenville, I approached this beautiful tree and asked her permission to set up my residence."

"You can speak to the tree?"

"I am advanced in the Art of Mischief, so yes I speak to trees."

"Amazing!" my mom's eyes were wide and so was her mouth.

"I believe that your next question pertained to the size of the tree. I am able to make her grow at will. I am able to make her shrink at will. As soon as you entered, I shrunk her back down to normal size. I knew you were coming, so I was ready. I wouldn't advise visiting much during the day though. Even though there are not many vehicles on this gravel road, they might notice if the tree at the end of the Hansen's driveway becomes behemoth."

I couldn't resist the question that formed, "What does 'behemoth' mean?'

"Young One, you need to start using the context of the sentence. What clues did I use in the sentence which might help you to help yourself?'

"I know. I know. It means huge. Just checking to see if you were on your toes."

As we reached the first large crook of the tree, the elevator stopped. We entered at the back of the house, and this floor plan was exactly the same as the floor-plan in Roxsthroe! We sat down at the table; while Ernst started his first of many chats with my mother, I explored more of the tree house.

Our first visit with Ernst went beyond well. My mother made Ernst laugh several times. At the conclusion of our visit, my mother asked, "Ernst, could Kip visit you? I think he wonders about the Art of Mischief, and, I must admit, I grow more and more curious as well.

In addition, I would feel safer for Kip if he learned some about this magic. His innate abilities coupled with the Art of Mischief would make him stronger against any evil. In addition, it would probably be helpful to him if he knew the history of Roxsthroe. In that respect, I wouldn't mind reading a book or two on the history as well. "

Ernst nodded in agreement and said, "Agreed. Kip will visit me daily for two hours and will learn the Art of Mischief as well as Roxthroe's history. This is agreeable. Patty," he called my mom by her name as if they'd known each other for years, "Kip and I are quite compatible"

I couldn't resist, so I asked, "Ernst, what does *compatible* mean?"

"In the words of your world, we are two peas in a pod," Ernst replied.

Laughter filled Ernst's treehouse that day and in the days to come. I studied eagerly, which made my mom proud of me too. During the regular school year, she would ask me what I'd learned and I wouldn't really care, but when she asked what I'd learned after a trip to Ernst's treehouse, I rattled off facts and figures and spells and strange stories as if I were a record player on the highest speed. As usual, her pride made her eyes sparkle.

Chapter 30

At the beginning of June, my cousin Vinny came to visit for one week. He lived in Pierre, a city-kid or a townie, depending on if you considered Pierre a city or just a town. Much of the time, Vinny and I found ourselves one-upping each other.

Ernst and I agreed that I should take a break from my lessons and that I should enjoy my time with Vinny. We determined that I'd not visit until Vinny had left.

Vinny and I had our customary list of stuff to do: we took our three-wheelers out on the farm tour, including a stop at the Rock (where I traced my hand along its middle and Vinny hollered, "What the heck are you doing to that rock?"); we shot B-B guns (but not at gophers); we swam in the dug-out and in the Faulkton city pool; we climbed hay bales; we built forts; and we created adventures of all kinds.

On day six, Saturday, we found ourselves in the backyard snacking on Skittles and juice. As we munched, Vinny stated, "Did you know that the green Skittles make you invisible?"

"Really?" I asked

"Yeah. Let's try it! Let's play Star Trek."

Before I knew what happened, we chomped on green skittles and raced naked across the backyard. I really thought Vinny might be right about the green Skittles until I heard my mom yell out the kitchen window, "Kip John Hansen! Vincent Sal Lahren! What the hell are you doing?"

I think Vinny was more embarrassed than I was because his clothes were back on his body in seconds. I felt sorry for him, too, because I knew that I wouldn't want my aunt to see me naked.

Once our clothes returned to our bodies, my mom came outside for the usual "talk." You know the one; it starts with "Now boys..."

After the talk, we sat back down on the step. I finished my Skittles because Skittles are a treat when you live thirteen miles from town. Vinny said that he had Skittles all the time. City-kids! While thoroughly enjoying my Skittles, I didn't realize that Vinny was upset until I turned my head toward him. His lower lip was a definite pout.

"What's the matter?"

"I'm not really having any fun," he said.

"Why?" I asked.

"I don't know. I'm kind of bored."

"Sorry. Do you want to shoot tin cans off fence posts again?"

"Nah."

"Do you want to swim in the dug-out?"

"Nah."

I let the silence settle in because I knew as well as he did that the city of Pierre had a ton more things to do. I'd been there for a week the summer before.

I didn't know what to do, so I just waited for him to talk, and I hoped that I could come up with something really fun to do.

Finally he spoke, "I wish green Skittles really did make you disappear. I wish magic really worked." Then he put his elbows on his knees and his chin in his fists.

The pause elongated like a piece of gum pulled from between your teeth, and during this pause, my brain turned. Should I? Shouldn't I?

I knew that I shouldn't, but I couldn't resist. I said, "But magic is real. Follow me."

About the Author

By trade Jeanne Hansen is an English teacher, and is in her seventeenth year of teaching English. She possesses a B.A. and M.A. in English, both degrees from South Dakota State University. She loves teaching, reading, and writing. Up to this point, she has written volumes of poetry and short stories but has never written nor published a novel.

Jeanne grew up on a farm near Lily, South Dakota. The rural environment fueled her imagination, and she began writing poems and stories soon after she read her first fairy tale!

Jeanne has three children, ages ten, seven, and six. To say that her children have influenced her writing is an understatement. Her ten-year-old enjoys fantasy books, and this, coupled with her family's love for the region where they have always resided, led her to a new endeavor. She has written books one and two of *The Rock Series* and currently works on the third book in the series.

The premise for the book began when she met her husband, Kip. He grew up on a ranch in Faulk country, near the Orient Hills. In the middle of his father's pasture is an enormous rock, a glacial erratic. When Kip and Jeanne first dated, he told her about this rock and how he loved riding out to it on the three-wheeler, how he loved climbing it, and how he loved playing on it. After they married, his dad and mom took Jeanne out to the rock. Kip was right; that rock was enormous!

As she approached 40 years of age, Jeanne decided that if she wanted to publish and thus cross off one item from her lifetime goals' list, she'd better start typing. She has spent the last three summers writing and revising. Now, thanks in part to the encouragement of many friends (especially Kay), Jeanne presents...her first novel.

Jeanne, Kip, Colton, Alana, and Lawson currently reside in Watertown, South Dakota. She works for the Watertown School District. Over the last nine years, she worked for Watertown High School, where she befriended the most wonderful students, colleagues, and administrators. Currently, she teaches English at Lake Area

Technical Institute in Watertown; and she continues writing the third book in this four-book series.